No Limits

An erotica

By Ross

Edited by Journey

Look What You've Done to Me

Looking into this hotel mirror thinking to myself, what am I doing here? After all these years, why haven't I grown up already? It used to be the thrill of the chase that kept me going, now it's like muscle memory, almost an addiction. Just something I end up doing before I can even wrap my mind around what is happening. It's gotten to the point where I can't even differentiate between the women that I deal with.

It's like they're all the same, all linked together by the same problems, all tripping over the same stumbling block.

ME.

I'm not even supposed to be over here, I have Denise thinking I'm out of town on business. This shit is spiraling way out of control. I used to always justify what I did by reminding myself that I have needs, but now that justification isn't quite holding up like it used to.

I knew she wasn't putting out until we we're married when I got with her, and I played the role thinking if I waited it out, she would eventually give in. Not a chance, she was true to her word and now I'm here again. I have to put a stop to this. Damn, how am I going to get rid of this broad?

Walking back out to the bedroom, mind working a thousand miles a minute, I paused. Stacy was sliding out of her sweats and T-shirt, slipping on a satin negligee that highlighted her long silky legs just right. My whole train of thought was jostled for a second, but I had to stay strong.

I put on a confused look and asked, "Stacy, what are you doing?"

"I'm just slipping on something sexy for you, are you going to come out those boxers or what?"

"Nah, not tonight."

She narrowed her eyes, walking towards me, "Playing hard to get tonight, huh?"

"Not at all, I'm just saying I didn't call you over here for that," I lied.

"Travis, its two o'clock in the morning. What else did you call me over here for?"

"To talk," I said, nonchalantly.

"To talk?" she responded in a questioning manner. After a moment's deliberation, she asked "Okay, so what's on your mind?"

Damn, I thought for sure she would have left by now. So, I spoke fast, "I want to talk about this, about what we are doing."

"What's there to talk about?" she said, "It's just sex."

"Not to me, not anymore."

Frustration starting to set in, she blurted out, "Nigga since when? What you done went to church and found the Lord or something?"

"Nah," I said keeping my composure.   "It ain't that, I just been thinking, why are you fucking me and you don't love me?"

Before she could respond I asked another question, "Even more importantly, how can you lay with a man that doesn't love you?"

Silence.

I'm thinking she's about to storm out of here any second, but to my surprise, after some thought, she actually answered.

Damn, Damn, Damn! I thought to myself.

"Well, to be honest, Travis, I like you. I think you're funny, you're very attractive, and you make me feel comfortable."

"Yeah, but I don't love you," I said.

She responded, "Since when you have to LOVE somebody to fuck them?"

"Since when you don't?" I retorted, surprising myself.

"You know what, Travis?" she said, "You on some ole bullshit right now, and I ain't got to sit here and listen to this shit."

YES!! I thought to myself.

"Oh, well the door hasn't moved anywhere, baby girl. The same way you carried your ass in here, you can carry your ass out!"

Packing her clothes in a rage, she's mumbling something unintelligible that I'm sure would have hurt my soul, if only I could decipher it. She stops and asks, "Where is this all coming from Travis?"

Damn, this broad is like a tree planted by the waters, she isn't going nowhere no time soon. Quick, I got to say something. *OK, got it.*

"Where's the condom?" I had a trick for her ass. I knew damn well she was depending on me to have them, like always.

"Why you acting brand new, boy?" she asked. "What, you don't have any condoms all of a sudden?"

Putting on like I might have forgotten, I said, "I thought I did."

As I was looking diligently for the rubbers, she blurted out, "Travis you know I trust you, right?"

"What you mean trust? Ain't that much trust in the world," I said, and continued on with the "search."

"I'm saying, you clean right?"

"Yeah," I responded. "What's that supposed to mean?"

"I'm saying, just this one time isn't going to hurt nobody right?" she said.

"Hell NO!! That's crossing a boundary I am not ready for," I exclaimed. "That's some shit you're only supposed to do with somebody you plan on marrying and starting a family with."

"Nigga, ain't nobody trying to have your kids or marry you. I don't know if I could even share an apartment with you, let alone marry your ass."

"Exactly" I said. "You see how fucked up this is now?"

She was puzzled.

"Listen to what you said, girl. You said, you don't even know if you could share an apartment with me. Yet, you want to share your body with me? Isn't your body more important?"

Silence.

"Would you not rather share an apartment with me first, share ideas and get to know each other, before sharing your body with me?" I was starting to feel the reality of the words I was speaking, and I think she was too, because tears started to well up in her eyes. I felt horrible, but not as bad as I would feel if I slept with her again. She came towards me, tears staining her cheeks, I embraced her.

She looked me in the eye, "Travis, you're right. You're absolutely right." She hugged me tighter. Her embrace felt good, I can't front. She smelled good too. I began to feel aroused. She looked up at me again, soft spoken she asked, "But can't you make love to me this one last time?" Reluctantly, I obliged. I think we both knew this was far from love. Just another sexual encounter.

The sun's rays were blaring through the wide open curtains. I told Stacy time and again not to leave them open like that. I hate waking up to the bright ass sun! I am not a morning person. I'm never fully awake until 10am. Shit. Reaching over to her side, I noticed the bed was cold.

I guess she got the hint after all. *Damn, no good bye? No last words? Nothing? Oh well, less stress for me,* I thought, as I stepped into the shower. Now it's time for me to get on home where I belong. I'm so glad this chapter of my life is finally over. *Now I can carry on in peace. No lying and sneaking around for me any longer. From now on, I'm a straight shooter*, I thought, as I began to sing "My Girl", in every key but the correct one.

Walking through the hotel lobby, I felt how Jennifer Hudson must feel singing that song on those weight loss commercials.   It was definitely a new dawn and I was definitely free.

"Excuse me sir," the bell hop interrupted my thoughts. I spun around on my heels. "Good morning to you," I said. "Morning, Sir. A young lady left you this envelope this morning." I knew Stacy couldn't leave without a word just like that. Whatever she had to say, I could do without hearing. On second thought, I guess I might as well see what she has to say.

I opened the envelope. The first page was mostly blank with a lipstick stain. Under it read, "Just think, I actually loved you." *This broad be fronting so hard,* I thought, shaking my head at her words. *I knew she was in love with your boy, the way I was putting it on her. Awwww shit, feels like she left me some parting flicks, hopefully she's naked in these… WHAT THE FUCK?*

My heart felt as if it took a swan dive to the floor, and now was racing back up my leg to repeat the jump all over again. Picture after picture of me and Stacy going into one hotel after another. *Oh my God! Why the fuck am I walking around with my hand on her ass like she is my woman?*

Finally, getting towards the end, another note read, "I'M IN THE CAR, DICK FOR BRAINS. GATHER YOURSELF TOGETHER AND TAKE ME THE FUCK HOME!"

Walking out the lobby's revolving door, I passed the valet, snatching my keys out of his grasp.

"Wow, no tip?"

"Fuck no!" I said. "As far as I'm concerned, you can go eat a bag of baby dicks!"

Slamming the car door shut, I took a deep breath looked to my right. Denise was sitting there, her big bedroom eyes bloodshot and wet with tears.

I opened my mouth, but I couldn't allow the words that sat on my tongue to be heard. She deserved better than to hear another lie. I couldn't allow what was blaring in my mind to be heard either. I thought for sure the truth of why I committed such an atrocity would crush her even more. So there I sat mouth ajar, unable to say anything.

"Don't just look at like a deer caught in the headlights! How can you do this to me?" she belted between sobs. "How? How?" she began to yell, swinging wildly and landing blow after blow on my back and arms.

"Would you stop hitting me, woman?!!!" Her punches finally subsided enough for me to start the ignition. Putting the car in drive, I lashed out, "How are you going to disrespect me like this? You put your hands on me; embarrass me in front of all those people? I'm supposed to be your man!"

"Embarrass you? Fuck you, Travis!
You're so fucking selfish!   Embarrass you?
I'm embarrassed, you asshole! You cheated on me!   Do you know how dumb I feel?   I tell everybody about you. Every day I carry on about how much I love you, talking their ears off about how much I thought you loved me. Telling everybody how good my man was!
Ha!" She began to laugh hysterically.

Damn I really fucked up this time, I thought to myself.

As her laughter slowly died out, she turned her face toward me, narrowing her eyes and pursing her lips, she said, "My dream man. But noooooo, you ain't no man. You're a coward, that's what you are."
I wanted to interject, but I felt she needed to get this off her chest.
Besides, at this point, anything I said would be held against me.

Walking into the house, I expected her to start packing my things and show me the door at any minute. Wow, what a day, and it's barely begun. Looking into the bathroom mirror, right into those eyes, trying to find a hint, just a glimmer of the man I used to be. No luck.

The steam from the shower felt so good, if only I could stay there until her anger dissipated. Okay, how am I going to right this ship? Flowers and candy will not be enough this time around. Hell, I'll be lucky if she lets me stay here until the lease is up.

"Open your eyes baby," Denise said, in a soothing seductive voice. Opening them slowly, unsure of what I was about to see, my mouth dropped. "Denise what are you doing?"

There she stood, in her pearl white silk lingerie, complete with garter belt and clear pumps.

"This is what you wanted right? You wanted a whore right?" Biting her bottom lip, she stepped into the shower and whispered in my ear, "You like slut's right? You don't want a goody two shoes that's waiting for marriage to give you her body. You want your pussy right now, right? You want everything you want whenever you want it? No if's and's or but's about it. Isn't that right?" she said as she began to bite my ear softly. Her hands slowly began to caress my enlarging manhood.

"You need to stop!" I forced myself to say. "You know you want to wait until we tie the knot. I can't allow you to do this!" She pushed me into the wall and looked me in my eyes, "Travis, you are not in control anymore." She stroked my rock hard penis, grabbed around my neck and said, "Now I want you to take this big ass dick of yours and take me from behind."

"You sure that you…"

"What the fuck did I say?" She interrupted, and stepped out of her negligee.

Turning her back to me, sticking out her big, succulent ass cheeks, "Go ahead, fuck your slut, and take what you want like you always do." I couldn't hold back any longer. I began to wrap her hair in my hands and slap her ass. "Yes that's right! Is this how Daddy does his whore? Spank that ass daddy!" I began to kiss the back of her neck slowly. Her talking turned to hushed moans. Simultaneously rubbing her clit, I slid a finger into her tight honey pot, nice and slick. Turning her face to me, I began to kiss her softly as the head of my manhood began to graze her lips. As I slid inside her slowly, she looked at me and said, "Fuck me hard Travis." "Baby, you're a virgin, I want your first time to be…" "Fuck me hard, I want it to hurt!" she interrupted, "I want the pain!"

I continued on slow, but steadily inching my way in, as I was before. Putting her left leg on the tubs arms rest; she thrust her hips back, forcing my insanely hard dick deep inside her. She buckled from the pain, biting her lip to refrain screaming. "Fuck me hard, Travis!" she said. Succumbing to her wish, I grabbed her around her neck and began to demolish her inner sanctuary.

"Oh My God! Fuck me harder!" she yelled, teetering the thin line of pain and pleasure. She began to dig her nails into my forearms, "Please don't stop!" I began to pump harder. "I'm about to come baby," I said as I felt myself losing control.

As I began to release deep within her, I felt her body tense then shudder all over. Holding her tight against my chest, we both watched the crimson creek of her innocence flow into the waterways that lead to the sewer. Turning around slowly, I lifted my head up so she could look me in my face.

"I wanted this to be special. I wanted this to be the consummation of our union. You took that from me," she said, as the tears rolled down her face. "Look at what you've done to me."

Bones in the Closet

"It has been three years since I have seen, heard, or touched Denise. She's the first thing I think about when I awake, and the last thing I think about before I retire for the night. It's like I just can't let her go Mike, you know what I'm saying?"

"Yeah man, I hear you."

"Man, you don't hear me, man. When have you ever been in love? I've known you all your life and I can't recall when you ever committed to one woman."

"Hell, Travis, I can't recall when you ever committed to a woman either!"

"You trippin'. Let me see, there was Shawna, Jane, Tammy and Denise."

"Travis, do you hear yourself?"

"What? You know those relationships were legit. Not like your hoochie-chasing ass!"

"Travis."

"What Mike?"

"Dude, you cheated on all your girlfriends!"

"But I tried to…"

"No excuses man, you are a cheater," Mike interjected, "Face it, own up to it. You are not loyal, and you are nowhere near committed."

"Hold up, who died and made you Dr. Phil, Brotha?" I retorted.

"I'm not trying to come off like that, I'm just saying what I feel is the truth.
Granted, I'm guarded, I know this. I will probably never bond with a female on an emotional level. Because of that fact alone, I refuse to play with their emotions. I know that I will be no good to a woman relationship wise," Mike said.

"Man you're just afraid to try, Mike."

"That may be true. If me failing means ruining a woman for the next man, a better man than me, I can live with avoiding the situation altogether."

"Man we got issues," I said.

"Now that's something I can drink to," Mike said as he raised his glass. Raising my Hennessy on the rocks, we rendered a salute in agreement.

"I been doing some thinking man, I'm really considering counseling."

"Counseling?"

"Yes, counseling," Mike said. "Maybe you should consider it, Travis."

"I don't need no damn counseling, Mike! No Sir! I can't see myself telling all my business to a person I barely know. No sir."

"Well, you have to tell someone. That is a lot to live with, man. Especially in your predicament, Travis."

"My predicament?" I said, laughing, "What would that predicament be, since you know so much?"

"You are a sex addict, Travis," Mike said.

The words hit like a short powerful strike to the solar plexus. I laughed it off, "Sex addict huh? I'm a man with a normal sexual appetite."

"Are you?" Mike asked.

We were eye to eye, man to man. I never thought of it as a character flaw, maybe he was right.

"You know what Mike, why the hell not? I'll try it just to show you how stupid I think of all of this is."

"Deal," Mike said, raising his glass.

"Deal," I said, as I raised my own.

Little did Mike know, I was already seeing a shrink.

"Good Morning, Mr. Marks. Please take a seat."

"Good Morning, Dr. Carter."

Looking around her office, I thought to myself, *there is no way this woman has read all of these books*. From floor level to the ceiling, nothing but books on top of books. I was impressed. Everything about her seemed very orderly, as if she lived life by a check list. Interrupting my thoughts was her punctual, yet sultry voice.

"So what exactly is it that is ailing you Mr. Marks?"

"Wow," I said, taking in a deep breath, "I don't know exactly how to say this."
"Just relax and speak, say whatever it is that is on your mind."

Reluctantly, pushing out my words as provolone is pushed through the grater, I mumbled, "I think I'm addicted to sex."

"Excuse me? I didn't quite get that."

"I think I'm addicted to sex," this time, blurting it out.

"See, was that so hard?" She said, with the most beautiful set of teeth I have ever seen, housed by a pair of lips that were screaming "kiss me."

"First things first, I would like to congratulate you by making what is the first of many steps to finding a solution to your perceived dilemma. To get a better understanding of your situation, I will have to ask you a series of questions regarding your sexual history, secrets and hidden desires. Are you comfortable with that?"

Thinking to myself, *hell, I'm already here, might as well let it out.* Sighing, I said, "I'm all ears Doc, ask away."

"When did you lose your virginity?"

"I officially lost it at 18. However, I was dry humping and kissing as early as 11 years old.

"Tell me more," she said, with a seductive smile.

"My first partner was experienced, she taught me everything," I continued.

"How old was this woman?" Dr. Carter asked in a rather calm voice, considering the topic.

"She was 26 years old I think."

"So how did it happen? In detail."

"In detail?" I asked.

"Yes, in detail, please."

"Well, at that time, I was a ward of the state. Every summer my foster parents would take a trip to Tennessee for a two week church convention. In their absence, Sister Meeks was asked to house sit and look after me. I really had a crush on Sister Meeks. She was my height, about 5'10, light skin, greens eyes and nice big lips with a button nose. Her eyes looked as if she always knew something you didn't know. With all of that said, that isn't why I crushed on her."

"Why did you crush on her?"

"I was so turned on by her lower half. She had virtually no stomach, wide curvy hips and her butt was big. Really BIG.

When I came down stairs to hug my foster parents goodbye, she was in the kitchen getting food ready.

Sometime after they drove off, she said, 'Come here and give me a hug boy', but her front half was to the stove.

"'Sister Meeks, how can I hug you, you are turned away from me?'

'Simple, sweetie, hug me from the back,' she said. I didn't think anything of it, but when I hugged her, I tried my best to keep my lower half away from her.

She then reached back, grabbed me by my elbows and said, 'A man has to hold a woman tighter from the back,' and pulled me closer until my penis was hard and erect against her big soft cheeks."

Shifting one leg over the other and clearing her throat, Dr. Carter asked, "So how did that make you feel?"

"It felt good physically, but I was embarrassed that she felt my hardness against her. So, I left abruptly, heading upstairs."

"What happened next?"

"Well, my dick wouldn't go down, and by now, I had developed this habit of masturbating whenever I was anywhere by myself. So I began to stroke my dick slowly."

"Were you thinking about Sister Meeks?"

"Most definitely. I always thought about her when I stroked it.

About 5 minutes or so goes by, and I hear her say, 'You have a pretty big dick to be so young, baby.' I opened my eyes, and tried to put it away, but she had already had her hands around the base of it. That's when I noticed she was

21

naked. She took over stroking it for me and started to whisper in my ear."

"What did she say?"

I noticed Dr. Carter's voice was getting a little softer.

"She was telling me that she was going to train me to be a real 'dominant man'. How to fuck a woman right. How to use my dick, tongue and mind to not only discipline, but to reward.

Little did I know, she was training me to be what she called a Dom."

"So Sister Meeks was into BDSM?" she asked.

"Yes, apparently so."

"Strange sexual appetite for a church going woman, but continue, Mr. Marks."

"So, she told me to grab her by her neck, look her into her eyes, and tell her to 'suck my dick bitch.'"

"WOW! Did you?"

"At first I refused. Pleading, she said, 'Please daddy,' and placed my hand on her soft ass cheek, near her now wet vagina and sat back slowly on my fingers. I began to feel her moistness."

"And is that when you obliged, Mr. Marks?"

"Yes. I told her, 'Gag on this dick, bitch,' and she shook her head no.

I was confused.

She said: 'When your sub refuses to do what you ask, you grab her hair a little tighter, not for pain, but for control. You take the tips of your fingers and give her a slap. It's not to cause pain, but to get her attention. Once you get her attention, you kiss her slow, deep and passionate, and you tell her again.'

That was the first lesson. She sucked my dick and swallowed my cum when I mastered it. Then she put what looked like a dog collar and leash around her neck. She had me hold it tight while she rode me. As she rode, I noticed every now and again she would shake. I didn't know at the time, but she was having orgasms.

When I got ready to cum, she rode it faster, assured me she was on birth control and I came inside her.

Every day all day, for those two weeks, we were having sex and she was teaching me new things. One group of lessons was for everyday sex with typical females, the other for what she called herself, a 'sub'."

"Oh my! Mr. Marks that is a lot to digest. So what are you thinking, now that you finally got that off your chest?"

"I'm thinking of masturbation."

"Really? So, the thought of Sister Meeks still makes you want to touch yourself."

"No, Doc."

"Call me Jane, Mr. Marks."

"Well, this time, I want to jack my big dick and think about you."

"Mr. Marks, that is highly inappropriate," she said, reaching fast for her phone.

Damn! I thought, *is she about to call security?*

"Doc," I said, "I apologize if I offended you…" she raised her hand to cut me off. "Sara. Sara!! Listen, I want you to cancel my next two appointments. This is going to take longer than I thought. Ok, thank you."

Hanging up the phone, she took the pin out of her hair and began to undress. I watched in amazement. She was a 5'9", hazel-eyed brunette. Nice big perky breasts, tight abs and a big bottom. She crawled over to me, stood up between my legs, looked me in my eyes, and said, "Your secrets are safe with me," while taking off my tie. Tying it around her neck in a knot, she handed me the loose end, saying,   "I want to be your little slut," as she knelt between my legs, pulled out my dick and began stroking it.

"Is that right?" I said.

"Yes daddy."

"I'm not sure how this is going to help me in the lonnnggg ruunnn," I said, shivering slightly as she began to slurp on my man hood.

"Mr. Marks, I feel you need to act out these urges, to see if this is part of you, or something that manifested because of your incident," she said, in between gasps while taking mouthful after mouthful of me.

"On one condition."

"What's that, Daddy?" she said.

"Open your fucking mouth and gag on this dick, bitch!" I said.

As she began to open her mouth wider, I slid my dick deeper.

This was how my sessions continued with Dr. Carter. I would come in, she'd welcome me as if she had never seen me before, we would then engage in some kinky, off the wall dirty talk, and commence to fucking like there was no tomorrow. Life was good for both of us. Not many shrinks can say they get the fucking of their life once a week, and not many patients can say their shrinks pay to see them.

Pulling my wet dick out of her mouth, I stood her up and began to slap her big, juicy ass over and over. You'd think I'd be used to it by now, but I'm still amazed at how big her ass is for a white woman. Must be something in the water nowadays.

"YES BABY SLAP MY ASS JUST LIKE…" putting my hand over her mouth, I rammed my dick into her pussy, nice and rough, just as she likes it. She begins to bite my hand as my other hand is around her throat. Her sweet tunnel spilling over with excitement.

I ask her if she's enjoying the pounding, she looks me deep into my eyes and lets out a long moan. I take a handful of her hair, wrapping it carefully around my fist, placing my other hand on her lower back I begin to stroke her slow and deep, just as she likes it, before she cums.

"I want something new this time."

"What's that?" I said, secretly hoping it wasn't more time. I still had one more client, and I could tell I would need a serious nap after this session.

"I want you to cum in this pussy."

Just the thought of it almost made me lose it, I had to slow down and start counting my strokes.

"I'm not… I'm not going to be able to do that," I said.

"I'm on the shot, don't worry," she said.

"So fucking what?" I said. It was growing nearly impossible for me to hold back my orgasm. As she leaned back and began to rub my head she whispered in my ear

"I'm paying for this big dick right? You better come in my pussy."

"Speaking of pay," I said between strokes, "I'm going to need extra."

"DONE!" she said. Now fuck me nice and steady with that big black dick. MMMMMHMMMM, just like that!"

"I'm about to explode baby!"

"Hold it a little while longer, I'm about cum!" she said.

I began to hit harder and deeper. Soon, she began to squirt on my dick.

I let it go.

"That's right, Daddy. Fill this pussy up! MMMM."

She began to cum again as if my orgasm was so good, it made her have one. After letting go what I thought was the last bit of man juice I had in me, she began to suck the rest out, slowly, with a devilish purpose until my cock was back up and ready.

"Slide that big dick in me one more time," she said.

"No!" I said laughing. "You do this shit every time I got to go," I said, half chuckling.

"I know," she said with her lip poked out, "You got to run and give my good dick away." I let her get away with calling it hers, what harm was she causing? We both knew the truth. Bending seductively over her desk, pen and check book in hand, she asked, "How much do I owe you?"

"Eight hundred."

"Eight hundred?" she asked.

"Yeah, Misses 'I'm on the shot', just in case you aren't, we will already be set."

"I ain't got to lie to your ass," she said.

"Funny how the South Philly accent come out after some good dick," I said, laughing.

"Kiss my ass," she said, while playfully bending over.

I kissed the left cheek, grabbed my check, and got the fuck out of there.

Making it to my car, I cut the A/C on full blast while reaching into the arm rest for my phone. I never took my phone in with me during a session, their time is their time. I wanted it to be completely about them. Checking my messages, I noticed Candace canceled on me, which was a letdown and a relief, all rolled into one. Yes, I was losing fifteen hundred dollars, but after my last session, I don't think I would have survived Candace. She is insatiable. A beautiful, wild, black and Dominican BBW. About two hundred pounds solid, a little tummy, but ass and tits for days. Sexy Latin accent, very submissive, like I like them.

My dick began to rise thinking about her, but the soreness made me quickly forget the Latin nympho.

Pulling up into my drive way, I got a call. Local area code, however, the number was unfamiliar.

"Hello? Can I help you?"

"Is this Mr. Travis Marks?"

"Yes this is him."

"Hi, I'm Miss Jacobs. I'm calling at this hour because you were referred to me by a friend. I have need for your talents and was hoping that I could see you soon."

"How soon did you have in mind?" I asked.

"Now," she said, in a rather stern voice.

"I'm sorry, I'm not going to be able to now, I just got..."

"I'll pay you double for tonight," she interjected.

"That sounds really enticing, ma'am, but I normally have a sit down with my clients to discuss wants, dislikes, insecurities, safe words and..."

"Basically, you want to see how I look," she said, "I'm about to hang up and Facetime you."

She calls back video call and she's standing there naked... flawless. Milk chocolate skin, natural hair free-flowing, nice C- cup breasts, stomach flat and tight which transitioned well into strong thick thighs and calves. When she turned around for me, it was like heaven, her ass set up like two perfect girl-sized basketballs.

I had made up my mind.

"Do you like Mr. Marks?"

"I do."

"The address is 4121 Flowerfield Lane. The door will be open. Let yourself in, undress at the door and proceed upstairs to my bedroom."

"Which room is your bedroom, Miss Jacobs?"

"The whole top floor is my bedroom, Sir. How long will it take you to get here?"

"About thirty minutes," I said. Really, the GPS was telling me 12 minutes, but I didn't want her to know we lived so close to each other.

"Ok, hurry up, Mr. Big Dick," she said, giggling, and hung up.

Hopping into the shower, I couldn't stop myself from thinking about how rude and aggressive Miss Jacobs was. Then I started thinking about her perfect figure and how I was going to fuck her into submission. I began to get excited just thinking about it.

When I arrived at her place, I was impressed. It was a nice gated community and from the looks of the cars in the complex, everybody seemed to be doing well for themselves. Walking up to her door, I began to knock, until I remembered she left the door open for me. I entered, closed the door behind me, and began to undress.

I was pumped!

"You don't even know I'm about to tear that ass up," I said, half smiling as I slid my boxers off.

I began my journey upstairs wondering, *why is it so dark?* Had I not seen the video earlier, my first guess would have been that I was being cat-fished.

I reached her room and noticed no one was there. *What the fuck?*

Checked under the bed. Nothing.

Let me take a look in the closet. Nope. Not in there either.

Wow, this chick totally wasted my time, I thought. As I turned to get ready to leave, all I saw was a gun in my face. "Who the fuck are you? And why are you naked in my house?"

"What?" I asked.

I notice her shirt read 'Chicago Police Department'. "I'm going to ask you one more time," she said, "Who are you? Why are you naked in my house?"

"Listen lady," I said, "You called me over here, you don't remember?"

"Sit the fuck down," she said, "Matter fact, lay the fuck down on the bed with your hands straight out where I can see them. With the gun to my head, she then began cuffing me to her bed posts. "I'll be back. I'm about to go to my squad car and call this in, fucking pervert."

Once she left, I began twisting and turning, desperately trying to slide out of those cuffs, to no avail. I heard her coming back up the steps, so I played cool, deciding that I would have to talk my way out of this. As she neared the door, I said, "Listen, I'm incredibly sorry…" I stopped short when I noticed she was butt naked, just standing in the doorway like a stallion.

Even though my life may have been on the line, I felt my dick rising. She crawled up my body seductively, gun still in hand. Tapping my shaft with the barrel of the pistol. "Who gave you permission to get hard?" she said, smiling while kissing on my neck. Working her way down to my collar bone, running her tongue along my chest to my navel.

She stopped, holding my dick in both hands, "You really do have a pretty big dick." Then she deep-throated it in one fell swoop. Pulling it out slowly, she giggled, "Oops, I'm getting a little ahead of myself. Let me slow down." She sat back at the end of the bed, pulling her panties to the side and began rubbing her clit counter clock wise.

"Do you like that?" she asked.

"Hell yeah."

"I know you do. I'm looking at how hard I got your cock. You love this shit."

She began to pull her breasts out and lick them with her freakishly long tongue.

"Wrap that tongue around my dick," I said.

"I see you're a talker, aren't you?" she said, standing up on the bed.

"Since your mouth is so big, put it to good use and suck on my fat pussy," she said, as she pulled her panties off.

Grabbing the back of my head, she began to grind her pussy on my lips and tongue. Soft sensual moans emitted from her as she moistened.

"Damn, your lips are so fucking soft," she said.

I began to tease her, flicking my tongue on her clit slowly, in the same pattern she was rubbing it. "Ohh shit baby, don't tease me like that."

I kept right on teasing her.

"I said, don't tease me!" she said, grabbing the back of my head and fucking my face. "I'm about to cum!" she said, "Lick my clit real fast baby."

I began slowly, working my way up to full throttle, flicking my tongue as fast as I could. "MMMMMmmmm shit! I'm fucking cumming!" she said as she released, her waves splashing on my tongue and chest.

"Let me get that up for you, baby," she said, as she took that long tongue and began to lick my lips. "I bet you want to come on my face now, huh?"

"I would like that."

"I bet you would. In due time baby, but for now, let me get that nut up out of that dick."

"Aren't you going to un-cuff me?" I asked.

"Why would I go and do a thing like that?" she said with a giggle, as she began to pour baby oil on my dick. "I'm going to save you fucking the living shit out of me for next time."

Her hands were so soft, not to mention, I looked huge in those small hands. "Mr. Marks, I can't wait to have this thick, long dick in my pussy. I'm almost tempted to give you a sample on the first date," she said with a laugh. She began to stroke it slowly with one hand as she stuck her long tongue in my mouth. I sucked on it a bit between kisses. She began to kiss and bite my neck softly. "Cum for me baby," she whispered in my ear as she began to stroke it faster. How I wished my hands were free so I could palm that nice, round ass! I started to feel my orgasm coming. "Just stroke the tip," I said. "Make that

34

big dick cum for me," she whispered in my ear, as I shot my load everywhere.

She took my dick and began sucking it. The action felt so good, it was torture. After licking me clean, she said, "Now give me a kiss." I turned my head, "Don't play, Shorty." "I'm just fuckin' with ya," she said, as she walked out to the bathroom.

"You can un-cuff me now!" I yelled behind her.

"Oh yeah, I knew I was forgetting something," she mumbled, tooth brush in her mouth now.

Un-cuffing me, she said, "FYI, the gun wasn't loaded."

"Yo, you wild as hell," I said.

"Say you didn't have fun," she said.

"I'm not going to say all of that."

"Yeah, I know," she said.

"I'm about to go down stairs, get my things and let myself out, Jasmine" I said, while walking towards the door.

"Aren't you forgetting something?" she asked. I turned around to her waving her check book.

"Yeah... right, I am forgetting something," I said.

"I'm making it out to… what's your name again?" she said playfully.

"Marks, Trav Marks."

"She laughed, "Ok, double O negro."

I busted out laughing.

She walked me to the door, helping me get dressed. "I will be getting in touch with you again soon, I have a special mission for you, I hope you will be ready," she said, still alluding to the James Bond series.

I laughed some more, "I'll be ready."

"We'll see," she said, as she smacked me on my ass before closing the door.

WOW! What a fucking night, I thought to myself, as I reached my front door. *I'll take a shower in the morning, I'm beat.* As I unclothed and flopped into bed, like clockwork, Denise popped into my head. A bittersweet memory that I'm forced to have every night. I closed my eyes, and braced myself for the beautiful nightmare that was sure to attack my subconscious.

Hard Day's Work

Busy day today, I thought to myself, as I ran my hand through my closet, trying to pick the perfect suit. I have a 9 o'clock with Mad House Publishing to discuss a poetry book. After that, I have Sonya the house wife. I call her that because she likes to role-play that we are in a relationship, down to faux arguments and everything. Sometimes I really forget that we aren't together!

When I leave there, I have to make a stop at Jane's. Entertaining Jane was bittersweet, she reminded me of an Asian Denise. To make matters worse, like Denise, she is a lover of poetry. She's about the closest I've gotten to Denise in a couple of years. Principal by day, freak by night. The perfect woman.

I hate driving in the morning, and I kind of enjoy the train rides. Keeps me grounded, plus, I'm sure to see something I can get a good laugh at. I really hoped Mad House would decide to pick up my book. I've been sitting on this material for years, waiting on the right opportunity to come along the way. *It's my time*; I had to keep reminding myself. Looking out the window at what used to be the Ida B. Wells, State Way Gardens and Robert Taylor Homes. More and more this city is changing. *Chicago is starting to get a little too big for its britches,* I thought to myself. Arriving at my stop at State and Lake. I did a couple fake punches, to release some of the anxiety, "Let's go get 'em," I said to myself.

Sitting across from Mr. Stanley, Head Editor of Mad House, feeling hungry. The man was skinny as a rail. Balding slightly, pale white skin, blood shot eyes, from drinking all night, presumably. He may not know anything about fashion, judging by his choice of clothing, but he sure knows how to sell books. He whirled around in his chair, looking at me over his taped-up, wire-framed eye glasses, He said, "I have some good news, and I have some not so good news."

"Give me the good news," I said, dreading what could possibly be the bad news. "The good news is we are going to pick up your book, Mr. Marks." *That's what the fuck I'm talking about,* I thought, while doing a Tiger Woods fist pump.

"Ok, Mr. Stanley, give me the bad news. Hell, I'm ready," I said smiling.

"The bad news is, we want you to think Global. You know, big picture."

"That's not bad, man," I said, still smiling, "What do you have in mind, exactly?"

"We noticed, outside of your love poems, which are phenomenal, might I add, I mean really Grade A stuff." *Get on with it, spit it out I thought to myself.* "We came to the conclusion that the book is maybe too Afro-centric."

"Too Afro-centric"? Hold up, Mr. Stanley, I came to Mad House because you are the leading publisher of Black material."

"Yes, this is true, Mr. Marks, but have you ever read any of that material?"

"Well, no, I can't say that I have."

"Well, I'll tell you now, it doesn't hold a candle to your literary expertise. However, it is what the people want. Trav, can I be blunt?"

"Sure."

"I'm not trying to sound like a bigot, but Black people don't want to read about the trickled down effects of slavery on the Black man in America today. They want to read about money, sex, murder and deceit. Take a look at your average romance novel nowadays Trav, it's just soft-core porn printed on paper."

"So what are your suggestions?"

"Our suggestion is that you make slight adjustments to your wording to make the book more appealing to a wider fan base," Mr. Stanley said.

"What kind of adjustments?" I asked.

"Oh, simple things, like for example, instead of saying "Black Queen," say "Woman." Just make it a general statement that covers all women. We don't want potential buyers to feel left out of the loop."

"What if I told you that I want my book to stay as is? I put my heart and soul into that book, any modifications to it would be like me reaching inside my own chest and casting away my heart! Mr. Stanley, I thank you for the opportunity, but I have to decline."

"Travis, don't make a decision in haste. Sleep on it," Mr. Stanley insisted.

"I've made up my mind. If that be all, I will see myself out."

"Well, Mr. Marks, I cannot say this offer as it stands will still be on the table if you walk out that door," Mr. Stanley sternly advised me.

"I'm sorry Sir, but this book is MY LIFE! I cannot change it, not even to make a few extra dollars," I said as I walked out of his office.

Finally reaching my place, I thought to myself, *the old bastard has a point.* Generally, Black people aren't into the whole Black Power, Black Is Beautiful-type message. I just couldn't sell out my dream, rearrange or discard parts of my life for a buck. Had he asked me to write a separate book, a book more relatable to pop culture, I might have considered. Oh well, what's done is done. Life goes on, and I still have a whole day's work ahead of me. Speaking of work, Sonya is definitely going to get this work today! With all of this pent up frustration in me, she is in for the fucking of her life.

"Trav! Trav! Travis!"

"Huh? Oh, what's up, Mike?"

"Why the fuck you in here dressed like a construction worker?" Mike said.

Looking down at my coveralls, safety goggles, steel toe boots and hard hat in my hands, I couldn't do shit, but laugh.

"Mind your business, Mike," I said, holding in laughter.

"Nah, Brother I NEED TO KNOW!" he said, half laughing himself. "Because I came in here to get my daily turkey on wheat and 'Eat Fresh', I look to my left and see you over here trying to blend in with the blue collar folks."

I decided to tell Mike the truth, well, most of it.

Sighing, I said, "If you have to know so badly, I'm about to entertain a lady friend."

"Dressed like that?"

"Yeah, dressed like this."

"What you about to show her, how to lay plywood?"

I busted out laughing, the White lady ahead of me turned around to see what the fuss was about. I just continued laughing as if she wasn't there.

"I don't know brother, there may be some wood being laid," I said in a matter fact manner.

"Maybe? She got you out here looking like this! You better be getting some ass!"

We both were crying laughing now.

I paid for my food, dapped up Mike, and shot out of there. Maybe, just maybe, I could tell Mike the truth about what I really do. It feels kind of bad lying to my friend. Even though, what I do for a living is my business. It still feels wrong; I remember when I used to tell him everything.

Man, I didn't feel like dealing with Sonya's shit today, but the sex was phenomenal, and the money, even better! After a couple of knocks, Sonya answered the door hurriedly, stopping to give me a quick kiss on the mouth, she said, "Hurry up, Daddy. Your food is almost ready. Get those stinky clothes off babe. I'll be in the bathroom to wash you up, right after I take the chicken out of the oven." Watching her speed walk back to the kitchen was a sight to see. She was about 5'3, STACKED! Double D cups, tiny waste with about a 46 inch ass. I know personally because I got bored and measured it one day. She wore her hair natural, a nice and kinky, wild afro. Brown, almond-shaped eyes, high cheekbones with a set of full, kissable lips. If it wasn't for her smart ass mouth, she wouldn't have to role play having a husband, men would be literally beating the door down to get to all of this.

The warm shower water felt good running down my back.   I opened my eyes in just enough time to see her peeling out of her boy shorts. Each cheek took a nice bounce as she got the shorts over her pear-like hips and slid out of them. She noticed me looking in the mirror, so she slowly took off her bra, giving each of her nipples a soft, sensual kiss.

Stepping in the shower, she said, "You could've at least started washing up. Damn, I got to do everything for you. Cook, clean, and wash your ass!"

"Sonya, did you not say, go to the bathroom, and you'll be coming right behind me to wash me up?"

"I know what the fuck I said! But still, you could have at least started by now. And you left your fucking clothes in a big pile by the door. I guess I'm your maid too! I swear, I don't even know why I still fuck with you after all of these years. It's clear you don't appreciate shit I do!" She said, while lathering my body up with soap.

"You don't know why you fuck with me?" I said. "Maybe you fuck with me because I bust my ass every day at that construction site trying my best to make a living," I said sternly. "Or maybe, you're just typical, and deal with me for this," I said, as I grabbed my dick.

She slapped my hand away, "Give me that," she said, as she began to carefully clean it. I swear, she had a gift. She was the only chick I knew that could piss you off to the fullest, while at the same time making you feel on top of the world. If only she knew the former wasn't necessary. "Trust me, it ain't the dick. I could get good dick whenever I want," she said, confidently.

"What the fuck you say to me?" I said. It turned her on when I acted aggressively, especially when the aggression was an expression of jealously.

"You heard what the fuck I said! I don't know why you're getting loud; you and I both know you ain't about that life."

"Oh, I'm not?" I reached out and grabbed her around the neck as she was about to step out of the tub. I pulled her back, making her face the wall of the shower.

"Bend the fuck over," I said, with my hand around her throat. I had a nice firm grip, not tight enough to choke her, but tight enough to let her know I was in control.

"Why the fuck you always talking shit?" I asked, as I slapped her ass really hard.

She let out a load moan.

"Answer me," I said, as I slapped her ass again.

"Because… because I want your attention, Daddy."

"And you don't, *SLAP* know any better, *SLAP*, way to get my attention?" I asked, as I ended with a nice hard slap on the left cheek.

She let out another moan and tried to reach for her pussy. I slapped her hand away.

"Did I fucking tell you you can play with that pussy?"

"No.

"No who?"

"No sir," she correct herself.

"That's better," I said as I began to caress the big juicy ass I had just assaulted.

"I got a trick for you," I said.

"What is that?" she began to ask, but I had already slid all nine and a half inches in her before she could get the words out.

"Daddy, what about the food?" she asked.

I put my right hand over her mouth, and my left hand on the small of her lower back.

"Shut the fuck up and take this dick," I said, as I began to fuck her hard and steady.

I tilted her head back so I could see her eyes rolling into the back of her head. That was my signal to go in slow and deep, just how I know she liked it. Whenever she would come to and look me in my eyes, I would go back to pounding her pussy hard and deep again, until her eyes would roll.

I didn't want the food to get cold, so I had to force myself to cum fast. I found myself thinking about my encounter with Jasmine. How bad I wanted to fuck her. I found myself fucking Sonya hard and fast. I heard her cry out as her warm cum dripped down my dick. I titled her head back so I could kiss her. "Yes, Daddy FUCK ME HARDER!!" I could hear her screaming in the back ground. But all I could see in my arms was Jasmine looking back at me, coming all over my big dick. I pulled my dick out as I began to cum. Sonya immediately got on her knees. I let it go all over her big, pretty, caramel breasts, completely covering the left one.

"Whoa! Shit, I'm hungry now. Last one to the kitchen is a rotten egg!" I said, as I hurriedly got out of the shower, grabbed a towel, and rushed to the dining room.

"Travis, you ain't right. You could have at least cleaned me off."

I had a Facebook message, "Mr. Marks, I took off early, don't go to the school house, just swing your sexy self on by."

That I will, I said to myself.

While getting ready to respond, I noticed a friend request. Who can resist checking a friend request? It was Jasmine! *How did she get my Facebook page when I have it blocked?* I thought. My dick immediately growing hard, I accepted.

Ten seconds after I accepted, I received a message. "Travis, clear your schedule for tonight. I want you to escort me to a party later on."

"Can't do," I said.

"Why?" she replied, with a sad face.

"Well, I have a lot on my plate today. To add to that, I received some pretty bad news. I don't really feel like partying," I said.

"No worries, I know you will be drained from your day. We'll just make a brief visit, and then be on our way. Deal?"

As bad as I wanted to see her, I couldn't come off as too eager.

"Okay, okay. What is the dress code?"

"It's a costume party, be creative."

"What are you doing?" I asked. As I took off my shoes and pointed them towards the door, according to Japanese custom.

"Nothing, sipping on wine, while waiting on you" she said, as she gave me a tight hug. "Want some?" Putting her hand behind my head gently, she poured a little into my mouth.

"I love Sangria. Can you pour me a glass, Sweetie?"

"Sure thing," She said, while sauntering off.

Jane's home was always cozy and quiet, like a classy bookstore. She was a lover of books, specifically poetry.

"Here you go", she said, as she handed me the glass of wine. "Before you take a sip how about a kiss?"

She looked up into my eyes, "Black men are beautiful," she said, as she kissed me slowly, rubbing her hands up and down my spine. She stepped back and let her robe drop. As it hit the ground my cock rose. She bit her bottom lip and said, "I'll be in the room, assuming the position, waiting for you to whisper one of your sensual poems in my ear."

I began to drink as I watched her walk off. Those squats I taught her were doing her justice, because that ass was getting fat. One thing I loved about Jane was her work out routine. She lives in the gym. Thirty-four years old, but looks like she's nineteen.

Sliding in the bed with her, I took hold of her silky hair, putting it over her shoulder so I could kiss her neck. She reached back and grabbed my throbbing dick, and said, "Speak to my spirit."

As I began to recite my poem in her ear, she slid my pulsating cock deep inside her. As I stroked her slowly, I commenced:

"This poem is called Lustful Nights."

I reach over to dim these lights

I glance over to my left

Caught forever gleaming in your eyes

Urges to fast forward to the meeting between your thighs

I had to suppress

Hurried to undress

So I can slowly ingest you

Thoughts of loving and caressing you all day

Finally manifesting themselves in this display

Fingers navigate through the waves of your hair

You meet my stare

As I tell you to grab it

I kiss your ear lobe as you hold

What you rightfully own

Slowly, you control me

As I begin to taste your nectar

Pulling your hair back

I run my tongue up and down the nape of your neck

Slowly nipping at your collar bone

The palms of my weary hands find peace,

Resting on your inner thighs

The beast raging within me as I try to remain civil

Your soft lips meet mines, as my heart sizzles

Exploring your secret place, I stumbled across a flowing river

Which made me remember?

The thirst I had to quench

Placing both hands on your hips

Your panties I rip clean off

As hungry as I am for your taste

I begin with a kiss

Softly, slowly, like a resident of France

My mouth started to romance the lips

I miss the most

With every quiver I get a sudden surge

Coming forth from your river

  You curse me with love

Frantically pulling me up

You taste my lips as you guide me in

I try to go

Slow but deep like an intellectual conversation

Tired of waiting, you pushed me all the way into the raging waters

As I splashed in, the river surged a little more

I stroke through current steady, every stroke with purpose

As if my life depended on it

Finally I can see the shore

Our eyes meet as you tell me to come home

As I reach the shore I show you how much I've missed you

As I release to you all of the love you have given me."

At this point, her fingers are woven into mine as we lay there cumming together. We both have multiple orgasms, one after the other. The bliss subsides, she is sound asleep. My cock is still hard for her. The fact that my poetry turned her on so much turned me on.

Grabbing the money order off the coffee table, I was on my way.

A New World

I was kind of excited pulling up to Jasmine's house. I didn't particularly know why, but I was. As I got out of the car to walk up the pathway, Jasmine was exiting the house.

"Wow! You look great," she said.

"Likewise," I replied.

"Soooo, let me guess, Men in Black?" she said.

I laughed, "No, but really close."

"Who are you then?" she said, smiling.

"You better act like you know," I said, while twirling around, so she could get a glimpse of the whole suit, "I'm Double -O Negro."

We both started laughing hysterically.

"Boy, you are a trip," she said, as I open the car door for her.

Once I got in the driver seat, she said, "Travis, can I ask you something?"

"Call me Trav," I said.

"Trav can I ask you something"?

"Sure."

"I want to drive your car," she said, with serious look on her face.

"That's not a question," I said, "And the answer is, HELLLL NO."

"Ok," she said.

Putting a pill on her tongue, she said, "Trav, here, take this for energy."

Without thinking, I immediately went in for the kiss. Anytime I got the chance to kiss those big ass soup coolers, I was going to take it.

"How long should it take to kick in?" I said.

"Ecstacy takes about forty five minutes to kick in."

"Are you serious?"

"Yep!" she said.

"Here," I said, as I tossed her the keys, "Take care of my baby."

"I got you!" she said, as she climbed over the arm rest, into my lap.

Her big, soft ass felt good, but I just looked at her like she was tripping as I slid from under her to the passenger seat.

Pulling up to what looked like a huge mansion, I noticed I started to feel a little loopy, light, and really, really good. I looked to my left to see Jasmine take one of the pills herself. Putting on a crown, she said, "If you haven't noticed, I'm the fucking Queen." She leaned over and stuck her tongue in my mouth; we kissed for a while before exiting the car.

The two hosts handed us masks likened to the movie Eyes Wide Shut. They were both stacked, standing there, butt-naked. On the White girl's forehead, read 'slut'. On the Black girl's forehead, read 'whore'. Jasmine placed a leash in my hand that lead to a collar around her neck. She whispered in my ear, "I may be the Queen, but I'm your slut. And these," she said, grabbing the leashes connected to the hosts, "are my sluts." They both got down and began to crawl in front of us, big asses in the air. I started to get aroused. The living room led into an open bay where you could look up and see the moon. There were four levels. The first one, where we were at, was a long corridor of rooms with glass bulkheads. We could see them, but they couldn't see us. "This room is where men come to watch other men fuck their wives." From what I could see, it looked like about nine brothers putting the works on two white girls while two men watched.

"Are you serious?" I replied.

"Yes, I am Daddy. Whatever you are into, you can find it here."

The next room was like a mini strip club, there was a thick, dark chocolate goddess bent over, taking it in all holes, as a line of white guys stood around her waiting their turn. She seemed to be in heaven.

"Look in this one," she said.

In this room was an all-out orgy.   Multi-racial, about seven girls and five guys going to town.

"Ok, King," she said, this is our stop. The door read 'FMH Initiation'. As we walked in, I saw an assortment of different shades of chocolate, all of them voluptuous. From slim, to thick, to bodacious, all hips, ass and tits: BBW. Jasmine took off her mask and said, "Ladies, meet our prospective King of the Court". One by one, they stood up to greet us. They were walking right past the collared women as if they weren't there. Finally, one of the sisters spoke to them. "You two bitches stand over there, in the corner. Don't walk. Crawl!" The screamer introduced herself first.

"Hey King, I'm the Master at Arm's here. My duty is to take charge of all discipline, and make sure all meetings are conducted decently and in order. My fellow queens call me Boss Bitch."

"Nice to meet you, queen."

"Likewise, King."

They were all dressed in black boy shorts and pink t-shirts that read #FMH society on the front, and FUCK ME HARDER on the back.

From my left side, I heard a gavel slap wood. "Queens, before we feed our hungry pussies, we must commence the initiation. Boss Bitch, rounded up those two sluts. Bodacious, Make It Nasty: please remove the king of his clothes." Bodacious was what they called the Amazon, she was about 5'11, 220 lbs., all ass, tits and hips.

"Hi King," she said, kissing me on the lips while taking my jacket off. Deep Throat was down on her knees, kissing my inner thighs after she pulled my pants off.

"Ok, sluts, show us how bad you want in FMH. Suck that big dick of his real good. If you are able to make us horny enough to rub our pussies, y'all are in."

"Boss Bitch, see to it that their mouths get the fucking of their lives."

"I'm on it! You bitches get over here now! Get on your fucking knees right here! Here King, hold on to this," Boss Bitch said, as she handed me their leashes.

She then stood behind me, rubbing my stomach and abs and kissing my neck.

"Snow Flake, go!" Boss Bitch commanded the thick, blond-haired, blue-eyed White girl. Snow Flake took my big dick deep on the first try and began to fuck the back of her throat with it.

"Co-Co, lick those balls nice and slow, up the middle of the sack like you're eating a pretty pussy." The combination of the both of them had my dick at full capacity. As Snow Flake let me out of her throat slowly, I heard the cat calls from the gallery, most of them in hushed tones, all except Bodacious.

As loud as she could be, she said, "Damn, First Lady, you did good this time, because he got a big ass dick!"

Brushing off her shoulders, Jasmine arrogantly replied "I do what I do, and I do it well," while looking me right in my eyes.

Snow Flake started to get into it good, licking up and down the shaft then spitting on it.

"Hold the fuck up!" Boss Bitch said, getting face level with Snow Flake and Co-Co. "Did I tell you to spit on that dick, Bitch?" she said, while pulling the girl's hair.

Slapping Co-Co's face with the tips of her fingers, "Look at me slut. Did I tell this bitch to spit on his dick?" She shook her head 'no'. "I didn't think I did." She looked Snow Flake in the face and said, "You do what I say, when I say it, and how I want you to do it. Understand? Now open your fucking mouth and suck on his balls nice and slow," she told Snowflake. Co-Co wrapped those juicy ass lips around this dick and sucked it nice and slow. Standing up, Boss Bitch looked me in my eyes and said, "I can't wait to feel that big dick in my pussy," kissing my eyes, nose, then lips. She slid back around me and began to bite and suck on my neck as she was doing before. Co-Co was sucking my dick as if she were in love with it.

"Kiss each other while keeping that big dick in the middle," Boss Bitch said. I felt her rubbing her pussy behind me. Co-Co was such a turn-on, rocking her natural 'fro, no make-up, just lip gloss, flawless skin. Snow Flake was sexy too, like a thick ass, real life Barbie. I looked up and noticed that all the sisters of FMH were rubbing their pussies. Bodacious and Thick Wit It were bent over the sofa with their big, juicy asses in the air. Jasmine was furiously fucking herself with a small dildo biting her lip. When she saw me looking, she took the dildo out of her pussy and began sucking on it, slowly. Make It Nasty had one finger in her ass while rubbing her clit with one of those huge vibrators that looks like a microphone. I wrapped Snow Flake's hair around my hand and then I grabbed Co-Co by the back of her neck. I began to fuck their mouths as fast and hard as I could. Going from one mouth to the other. Despite the punishment I was giving out, neither of them threw up on my dick. "Damn, Daddy!" Boss Bitch said.

By this time, the sisters began gathering around Co-Co and Snow Flake, rubbing their pussies with reckless abandon. Super Soaker went first, squirting all over my dick and Co-Co's face. This made me get even more rough and nasty with the girls. Then Jasmine squirted all over them while doing a three way kiss with Boss Bitch and myself. Next up was Make it Nasty, who put her pussy one inch away from Snowflake's face. "Drink that shit up, Bitch," she said. That sent me over the edge; I came all in Co-Co's mouth. "AHHHH FUCKKKK!" I screamed as the nut just kept flowing. "Share the wealth," Bodacious said. Thick Wit It Chimed in, "Both of y'all come the fuck over here and spit that nut on this pussy, eat our pussies, and catch this squirt juice in y'all mouths."

Boss Bitch said, "I think it's time we sit the King on his throne. What do you say First Lady?"

"Hell Yeah, Bitch, my pussy is hungry as fuck," she said. "Come here, Daddy," she purred, as she led me to a nice plush lazy boy. "Have a seat here, King," Jasmine said as she straddled me and slid my dick deep inside her wet pussy. "How does that dick feel, First Lady?" Make It Nasty asked, while rubbing her pussy in circles. "Sooooo fucking goooood," Jasmine replied. "Set that pussy on my face," I told Boss Bitch. "First Lady, soon as that pussy settles on my mouth, spread those ass cheeks and stick that long ass tongue deep in her ass."

"Ohhh Fuck! I got next!" Super Soaker said. The sounds of Jasmine and I devouring Boss Bitch just gave my dick more strength. Not to mention the fact that Snow Flake and Co- Co were spitting my cum on Bodacious and Thick Wit It's pussies just to lick it back up. From the sound of it, they were driving their thick asses crazy.

"Eat that fuckin pussy, yeah, just like that, baby! Oooooshiiiitttt. That tongue in my ass feels so fucking good," Boss Bitch said.

"I'm cumming Daddy," Jasmine said.

"You better come on that big ass dick!" Boss bitch said, as Jasmine's pussy tightened and shot out its lust. I came deep inside of her. "Yes Daddy, fill that pussy up with that hot cum mmmmmmm!" "Get over here, bitch, I want to taste that shit!" Make It Nasty said. As Jasmine slid off, Boss Bitch slid right down on it, her pussy talking to me immediately. Super Soaker climbed on top putting her pussy in Boss Bitch's face. I slide my tongue in her ass. Boss Bitch went in, servicing both of us. Bouncing on my big dick, as she slurped all of Super Soaker's squirt juice every time she came.

And so the cycle went, until each one of the 'Fuck Me Harder' sisters came on my mouth or my dick.

I awoke, laying between Thick With It and Co-Co. Sliding my morning wood out of Thick Wit It. I got up to use the bathroom. I always hated trying to piss with a hard-on. *I need to check my phone,* I thought. "Looks like most of the girl's took off," I said, as I walked up behind Jasmine.

"Yeah, they have. They left something for you too, on the table there."

I couldn't see what it was from where I was at, but I assumed it was money.

"Travis, those bitches already talking about the next meet and greet that's a month away! You really made an impression."

"Is that right?" I said, smiling, "Last night was so much fun."

"Did you enjoy yourself, King?"

"I sure did. Hey, have you seen my phone," I asked.

"Yeah, it's right here. I was playing Tetris on it."

"Did I get any messages?"

"Just one," she said. "Some chick named Denise left you a message."

Do You Still Love Me?

"Denise! Quick, give me my phone!" "Is that sincere interest I hear?" Jasmine inquisitively asked.

The message read: Travis when you get this, text or call me. I really, really need to see you.

I wanted to call her right away, but looking around, I knew I couldn't do that.

Giving her a kiss on the cheek, "Jasmine, I got to split. I had a fucking blast, sweet heart; I'll call you when I get in."

"You do that," she said, with a hint of skepticism in her voice.

"Daddy, how you going to leave before giving me some of that good bar?" Bodacious said. She put my hands on her fat, plump ass, and started kissing me sensually.

"Baby, I want too," I said.

"Then take this pussy daddy," she said, as she took my hand, placing it on her moist pussy.

"Bodacious, I can't, but I got you, I swear," I said between kisses.

"Let the man go, he'll be back," Boss Bitch said, with a sly smile.

"Awwwww ok," Bodacious said, kissing me on the cheek. "Somebody gonna eat this fucking pussy then," she said, as she plopped on the couch and spread her legs and pussy lips.

I made a step toward her, and then caught myself.

"You're a fucking freak, Travis!" Jasmine said, as she led me to the door. "Go take care of your business, call me when you get in, ok?"

"Ok."

"Be safe baby," she said, as she kissed my cheek. "Oh yeah," she stuck out her hand for a formal hand shake, "Welcome to the Fuck Me Harder Society of Sexual Exploration and Social Advancement." I shook her hand a little longer than normal. "Go head baby, if you hurry, you might get back and find us still here fucking and sucking."

We shared a laugh as I made my exit.

Back at my place, I sat there, looking at my phone. I had attempted to call her three times, but just couldn't bring myself to do it. I wondered, *what does she have to ask me? Why now?* Just when I found myself getting over her, she pops back into my life, like a beautiful twisted fantasy. "Fuck it," I said, as I depressed the send button, unlocking chains attached to a fallen angel that is capable of destroying my whole world with the sound of her voice.

"Hello? ... Travis?   Hello…?"

"I'm here," I said.

"Hey there!"

"What do you have to tell me," I said, getting straight to the point.

"Not over the phone, Travis."

"Why not?"

"Well, I think an issue as serious as this needs to be addressed in person."

"Ok, so where do you want to meet?"

"How about our spot?"

"Our spot?" I played coy.

"What?" she said, laughing. "You forgot? Red No. 5!"

"Ohhhhh, you talking about the Red No."

"Yeah, Isaiah promotes there now."

"Little Isaiah?" I said.

"Little Isaiah is twenty two now, and he goes by Chi-GOAT."

"Chi-GOAT? What the fuck?"

"Chicago's Greatest Of All Time, that's what he says it stands for."

We both busted out laughing.

"He says he's going to hook us up."

"Cool, so what time you want to meet up?"

"Meet me there at around 10pm."

"Denise, don't you think 10 is too early? Nobody is going to be in there."

"That's perfect, less people to fight over the bar tender's attention."

"Let me find out you are an alcoholic," I said, chuckling.

"I'm not, but there's no way I'm going to be able to tell you sober."

"That bad, huh?"

"Not actually," she said, hesitantly.

"Ok, cool," I said, hopping in the shower. "I will see you there."

"Ok, Trav, see you there."

"Chi-GOAAAATTTTT!" I yelled, as Isaiah waved me to the front of the speed line. "What's up, my Nigga!" He said, as he pulled me in.

"So you and Denise trying to rekindle, huh?"

"I have no idea. She invited me out, I accepted, and I'm ready to get it poppin'."

"Well, here's your bottle of champagne, complementary of the house, and here's your bottle of champagne, complementary of me," Isaiah said, as he passed me two bottles, one being Cristal the other being Rose.

"Thank you, my brother. Say, is Denise here yet?"

"Yeah, she's in V.I.P waiting on you."

As we approached, I saw her, she looked really good, but she had changed tremendously. She used to be the hair pent up, dressy type. What I saw before me was a sexy tom-boy, the complete opposite. She had on a Chicago Bull's fitted cap, underneath that was her hair pressed into a doobie wrap, nerd glasses, a cheek piercing, a black halter top showing off perfect abs, a black pair of daisy dukes on that read 'juicy' on the back, finished with some black and red Air Jordan's.

Grabbing one of the bottles from me, she said, "Hey there, here take a shot with me." She had a sly smile as she poured my shot, then hers. I couldn't help but gawk at how thick but toned she had gotten. I was starting to feel really aroused.

"How has life been treating you?" I asked, as we sat down in unison.

"I have been good. I got my own hair salon now so I can't complain. How have you been doing though? I see you're looking good, and still dressing fly with your Prada loafers on."

"Well, I been writing and working extremely hard. That's about it."

"Yeah, Mike told me you into construction now," she said smiling.

"Yeah, all I do is lay the wood though." There was a brief silence until we both busted out laughing, for two totally different reasons.

"So what's up? What you have to tell me?"

"Why you trying to rush in to it?" she said, as she poured two more shots. "Relax,

Sweetie."

Scooting closer to me, drinking Cristal right out the bottle, Denise said, "You know what I miss, Travis?"

Taking the bottle from her and taking a swig, I said, "What's that?"

She said, "I miss that big ass d…" looking off, something caught her attention in the general population area of the club. "I can't stand that bougie bitch!" she said.

"Where?" I said.

"Right there, she said pointing! The tall, big booty bitch! Right there, the club owner," she said.

When the girl finally turned around, it was Bodacious' thick ass. Soon as she locked eyes with me, she smiled and headed over.

Oh shit, I thought to myself.

"Oh hell no, that bitch look like she on her way over here. It's like you be having a spell on these hoes," she said, looking at me with disgust.

"Hi Travis," Bodacious said, letting it be known she knew me on a first name basis.

"What's up, Liz?" I said, avoiding Denise's death stare, "So, I hear you own the place."

"It's true."

"That's what's up! I love seeing my sister's make it in this world."

"Well, I wouldn't say make it yet! We all know, you haven't made it until you have a King you can share your kingdom with," she said seductively.

"Clearing her throat, Denise said, "Can I help you?"

Ignoring Denise, still looking at me, she said, "Anything you want from the bar is on me. I got to run, see you later Travis."

"Got Damn! I see you still get around!" Denise said, with a scowl on her face.

"Nah, it's not even like that," I said laughing.

"Well, I ain't even going to hold you much longer. I brought you here to tell you Mi…"

"Hold up, Denise, let me say what I have to say first."

Drunk, and free of inhibition, I began to say the things I have been holding in for three long years.

I grabbed her hand and said, "Baby, I've really, really missed you. I know that things will never be the same. I know this. But, I promise, I will work my ass off, night and day, to make sure they are better. You still hold the keys to my heart."

Lifting her chin up so we could see eye to eye, I said, "I love you, always have, and always will." I could see tears starting to well up in her eyes. Wiping them away, I said, "I am sorry."

"Do you mean that?" she said, looking me into my eyes.

"With all my heart," I said.

She immediately began to tongue me down. "I missed you too, I missed you so fucking much," she said between kisses. Getting hot and heavy, we didn't come to our senses until she pulled out my raging hard cock.

She stopped, looked around, and said, "Fuck that, I'm about to get this dick."

Putting the monster back in its cage, she grabbed my hand and said, "Come on!"

Weaving through a sea of drunken attention seekers, we finally reached the women's bathroom.

"You not thinking what I think you are?" I said.

"Yes the fuck I am."

Sticking her head in first to peep the scene, she led me in, all the way to the back stall, stripped down my pants, and began to throat my dick.

The feeling was so over the top, my knees buckled a bit. Pulling it out slowly, she looked at it with admiration. "I miss this big ass dick," she said, as she spit on it.

"Slide that dick in my pussy."

I wasted no time, holding her hands behind her back; I began pumping slow, deep, and deliberate. I wanted to let her know how much I missed her with every stroke.

She looked back over her shoulder and said, "Look how you got that pussy leaking. Can't nobody fuck me like this! FUCK ME HARDER, TRAVIS!"

"Oooohhh Girl, I think somebody in there fuckin'," I overheard some chicks talking.

I slowed down, "you heard that?" I said.

"I don't give a fuck, baby, go hard, bust that fat nut on my ass!" she said.

Following her instructions, I began to pound her.

Next thing I heard was "WORLD STARRRRRRRRR! WORLD STARRRRRRR!" Two girl's standing up on the adjacent stalls filming us fuck while adding their ghetto commentary.

"Fuck them, baby," she said, looking back at me. "Get that fucking nut baby."

I grabbed her by her jawline and began fucking her as hard as I could.

"Damn girl, she taking that dick," one of the ghetto girls said. "Girllll, I'm feeling some type of way. Shiiiiddddd, I got next, Boo-Boo!"

"I'm getting ready to cum."

"That's right, Daddy.   Cum on that fat ass."

"Get that pussy, get it," she said, as her nails dug into me.

I pulled out and began shooting my load all over her ass.

"Well DAMN!" the ghetto girl said, "All That FUCKING DICK AND CUM! OMG! Girl, I can't wait to post this shit on the BOOK!" she said, referring to Facebook.

"Denise! Where the fuck you at? DENISE!!"

"Oh, shit," she said.

"Oh shit? Fuck you mean, oh shit? Denise!"

"WORLDSTARRRR!" the ghetto girls said in unison. "She over here getting the shit fucked out of her!" They said, laughing.

"What the fuck? Oh, hell no!!"

"Who the fuck you in here with?" he said, kicking at the stall door.

"Mike?!" I said.

"Travis?" he said, his voice a little less intense.

"Hold the fuck up," I said, pulling up my pants quickly and looking down at Denise, "What the fuck is Mike doing here looking for you?"

74

"No! No, don't go out there."

Opening the stall door, I said, "Why the fuck you come busting up in here asking for Denise like y'all together?"

"We *are* together motherfucker!"

"Y'all what?" I said, as I swallowed hard.

"Yeah, you couldn't appreciate what you had, so I had to be the man you weren't."

"How long has this shit been going on?" I turned around to ask her.

"Three years," he answered for her. "We started talking during the last month of y'all relationship. Tell him!" he yelled at Denise.

"I don't know what you talking about, Mike. Travis his ass is lying!"

"I'll tell him, we getting married. There you have it! Mike looked in the camera, BOOM I FUCKING WIN!"

At that point I lost it, punching him in his face as I pushed him, glass from the mirror flying everywhere!

Denise starting to scream, "Just stop it!"

"WORLD STARRRRRRRRR WORLD STARRRRRRR WORLD STARRRRR!"

"What the fuck you going to do Mike? We both know you not a fighter, you fucking snake," I said, as I spit in his face. He tried to rush me, I front kicked him back to where the mirror used to be. I stood over him and began punching and slapping him around as he cowered.

"You were supposed to be my man, my fucking ace!" *Wham!* "You go behind my back and fuck with my ex?"

Wham!

"Huh?"

Wham!

"SPEAK UP YOU FUCKING PUSSY!"

WHAM!

Club security rushed in and tackled me into the wall. I didn't resist.

Mike quickly got up and grabbed one of the shards of glass from the mirror and swung it at my face. I got my hand up at the last minute! The tip of the glass went right through my hand.

He pulled it out to take another stab. One of the bouncers put him out of his misery with two gut shots, one to the rib, and the other to the kidney.

We both were escorted out. Mike was thrown out on the curb, still immobilized from the kidney shot. The police were already waiting outside and began reading us our rights as they cuffed us. The ghetto girls were still filming us, until Bodacious stood in front of them and said, "Cut those fucking cameras off before I snatch a bone out of one of y'all bitches." Mike was put in the first squad car as I was getting lead to the second car. A Crown Victoria rolled up stopping in the middle of the street. Boss bitch jumped out "I got this one," she said, as she grabbed me and lead me to her car. "Watch your head," she said, as she sat me in the car, "I'll be back, Travis."

I watched as she went back, seemingly upset, barking at the 'blue and whites', our term for the cops who controlled the beat. She came back with a First Aid kit, sterilizing, and then bandaging my hand. "That should stop the bleeding until we can take you to get looked after."

Looking at the crowd, I didn't see Denise, she was nowhere in sight. Starting the ignition, Boss Bitch looked in the rear view mirror and said, "I got something to tell you."

"Hey, before you say that, I just want to say thank you, because I sure didn't feel like sitting in county until morning."

"Who said I'm not arresting you?" I looked up quick, to see her smirking at me.

"I'm fuckin' with you," she reassured me.

"Then why am I still in these cuffs?"

"I thought you liked being in cuffs," she said.

"I was there when you fooled around with Jasmine at the house." I noticed we were driving up to Jasmine's place. "I was recording y'all."

"Wait a minute, what?"

"Jasmine and I are an item," she said, as she parked the car.

"Jasmine is a private investigator, the guy whose ass you just kicked paid Jasmine to follow up on you. He was the one feeding your ex all of the details of what you were up to."

I shook my head in astonishment. *What the fuck is going on around here?*

"I feel like I'm in the fucking Twilight Zone!"

"She was coming home talking about how sexy you are and how she was feeling jealous of the women you were fucking on her stake outs. We began to film you fucking! It got to the point where we were masturbating to that shit daily, you got skills boy!"

She reached back for a pound; I just looked at her, emotionless.

"Oh yeah, you're still cuffed," she said, with a giggle, "To make a long story short, that is how we tracked you down to initiate you! We like you," she said as she un-cuffed me, "We really like you, Jasmine and I."

"Why do you share me then?"

"Our views on sex is different from others, while we won't fuck another man, we will fuck as many women as we want. You can either join us, or watch. So we, therefore, cannot tell you who you can fuck. We just ask that everything be out in the open."

My mind was blown; this shit was like a Real Life Zane book!

Opening the door was Jasmine, hugging me with her head down. "I'm sorry I didn't tell you, but I was just doing my job," the words shamefully fell from her lips. After she hugged me, she kissed Boss Bitch on the lips and said, "Be careful, Truth."

Truth kissed my cheek, and said, "Jasmine, he fucked up his hand pretty good, don't get too caught up and forget to take him to the hospital." "We won't," Bodacious said, stepping from behind Jasmine. "Besides, he owes me for a mirror." Truth laughed as she shut the door. All I could say to myself was, *Oh, what a night.*

Atonement

I woke up to text messages and missed calls galore. Appointments I had to make up, Mike and Denise copping pleas, talking about how sorry they were. *Fuck outta here!* Looking at my hand I thought, *that muthafucka tried to stab me in the face though!* He's known me since the third fucking grade. I know the pussy good, but GOT DAMN! It ain't THAT good. That's crazy, my ex and my best friend were about to get married. I really fucked Denise up, if she going through all of this just to fuck with my head, SMH!

Got DAMN!! Sixty messages on Facebook! One by one, I opened them. All of them are talking about the World Star video. One of my homies talking about, "You made it my nigga?" Even a message from Mr. Stanley that read, "Call me as soon as you get this!"

I hopped up, wincing from the pain in my hand, I dialed the numbers.

"Hello, Mr. Stanley?"

"We'll do it!" he said.

"Do what, Mr. Stanley?"

"Travis, we will publish your book, as is!"

"Don't fuck with me Stan!"

"I'm not screwing with you, Trav. Just one condition," Mr. Stanley said, "You have to write about your life as a Porn Star!"

"But I'm not a pornstar, Mr. Stanley."

"Yes, you are! That video has grossed over one million views overnight on World Star, and 1.5 million on YouTube. Your name is trending on twitter; it's now being used to describe a sexual encounter where a man succeeds in giving a woman multiple orgasms."

"Get the fuck outta here," I said.

"It's the truth, I swear to you! Here, I'll read one to you, by YaMommasaHoe2003, and I quote, 'My girl was acting up all day yesterday, I took her to the crib and Trav Marks that hoe. Now she in the kitchen making me chicken and waffles my nigga,' end quote."

"Stan, don't be saying nigga all willy nilly," I said, trying to be serious, "This is crazy, Mr. Stanley."

"So, what do you say? We've got the papers already drawn up. You'll get max promotion on your poetry book; you and I both know you will need it."

"Oh, you got jokes, huh? My shit is dope and you know it!"

"Precisely, that's the reason you are going to need max promotion. People don't want to use their brains, Trav, Anything but that!"

We both laughed.

"Ok," I said, "You got a deal, but one condition."

"Name it!"

"We change Porn Star to Male Escort."

"Why change that? Well I'll be damned, Travis, you son of a gun. Are you really a…"

"I got to go, Mr. Stanley," I cut him off with a smile on my face; "You have a deal."

"You got six months to push the book out! We will be starting promotion today for both books as soon as you get in here and sign the contract!"

"Six months?"

"We got to strike while the iron is hot, Trav! You know, after your stunt, there will be thousands of self-made videos of people trying to out-do you! We want your book out in the unfortunate case that one of them does!"

"Yeah, you're right, but six months..."

"Trav, I wanted to wait for you to get down here to tell you this, but you're getting a 150k advancement. You'll have your expenses covered, long enough to get this book off. We believe your skill and the topic, coupled with the buzz you have, will pull readers out in droves."

I was speechless.

"Six months, Trav," he said again, as he hung up.

I know he said I can buckle down and write the book, but I can't see myself going without sex. I just can't! I know I'll write about all my sexual encounters, I'll just change names and nationalities to protect client confidentiality.

It is so on!

First appointment for today was Candace, the insatiable pecan Puerto Rican. Her ass to hip ratio was cartoonish. I knocked three times on her door; she answered it in just a white tee that fell to the top of her hips, ASS OUT. She kissed me on my lips, as she grabbed my tie and lead me into the house. "What have you been up to?" I asked.

"This is what I been up to," I saw my video playing and her toys laid out. "I been here, so horny waiting for you, Papi. I want you to fuck me nice and rough, just like that."

"Just like that?" I asked.

"Just like that, Papi. Show me no mercy."

"Have you been a good girl?"

That's the question I always asked before I gave her what she loved almost as much as the dick: a spanking.

She shook her head no.

"Why not?" I said.

"Because, you were not here to keep me in line, Papi."

"Get the fuck over here," I said, as I grabbed her hair and began to unbuckle my belt. Grabbing around her throat, I kissed her slowly on her ear lobe as I took my belt and gave her a nice whap across the ass.

"Ohhh Papi! Don't stop, please don't!" she said, as her knees buckled.

"Suck on my tongue," I ordered, as I slid it in her mouth. I kissed her again softly, telling her how disappointed I was in her. When she promised not to be bad again, I gave her another nice whap across the ass and hips! With every

84

kiss I planted on her neck and lips, I gave her a whap across her ass. Once her ass cheeks were nice and rosy, I bent her over and poured warm baby oil all over her big ass and began to massage and kiss her ass cheeks softly. Working down to the back of her thighs, hungrily, biting softly, sucking and kissing on both of them. I gave her asshole and pussy a kiss before swiftly flipping her over, grabbed the legs where they bend, pushed her legs back to her elbows, and began to devour her. Licking from her ass to her clit, flicking my tongue on her clit softly then slurping on it, then slowly running the tip of my tongue back down to her ass, tongue fucking it the same way I planned on fucking it with my dick, nice and deep.

She was in a trance, speaking fluent Spanish. I continued on my rampage. Moving back up to her fountain of youth, I began to write my name on her clit with the tip of my tongue as I slid my middle finger deep into her ass, as slow as possible.

"Ay, Dios mío! Papi right there! RIGHT THERE! PLEASE DON'T STOP!" I felt her pussy contracting, she was on the verge of cumming. I suddenly stopped.

"Did I say you can come?" I asked.

"No."

"When do you come?" I asked.

"When you tell me to," she said.

85

"And when do I give permission?"

I ask."

"Have I ever said no?"

"No Papi, never."

"OK, then." I slid my dick deep inside of her. She began to bite and suck on my neck as I stroked her with careful precision.

"Can I have it my ass Papi?"

"Yes you can," I said, as I placed a kiss on her forehead.

I slid in with little pressure, *she must have already been working her spot before I showed up*, I thought.

"Fuck me real hard baby!"

I began to speed, up!

"Harder Papi!" I knew she liked pain, it made her cum harder.

I began to think about the betrayal of Denise and Mike, the more I thought, the harder I fucked her.

"Si! Si! Papi, dame lo! Fuck me… just... like… that!" she said, starting to whimper.

Knowing how much she liked to be teased, I slid my dick out and re-entered her pussy at a nice and steady pace. With my hand around her throat, I pushed my dick in her deep and held it there, feeling her pussy moisten up that much more on my shaft. Her pussy began to contract. "Papi, can I come?" she asked. "Yes, you can," I said, as I re-entered her asshole and began to fuck the life out of her. Pinning her hands behind her head. I pounded her mercilessly; tears began to roll down her face as she bit her lips and began to scream. She released like a geyser. Eruption after eruption shot out of her pussy. Seeing her in this state of bliss pushed me to my breaking point. I pulled out and began cumming all over her fat pussy. She began using it as lube bringing herself to yet another orgasm.

After coming down from her high, she said, "Papi, you deserve a meal," as she lead me to the kitchen. She sat me down while she warmed up a plate of arroz & gandules with a big ole pork chop on the side.

"This is right on time," I told her. "Why aren't you married?" I asked her.

"Soon as I find a man with dick as good as yours, I will be," she said, with a straight face.

I nearly fell over in laughter. She began to smile, and then joined my laughter too! After the comedic intermission, I continued to scrape the plate; this food was way too good to let go to waste.

After signing my contract and picking up my check for one hundred thousand, (I still couldn't believe it, ONE HUNDRED THOUSAND!) I decided to call Jasmine.

"Hey, Jasmine!"

"Hey."

"I got some great news girl!"

"Oh, Ok," she said, nonchalantly.

"What's going on with you? Talk to me?"

"That little bitch Denise, that's what."

"What happened?"

"Well, if it is not enough that I got to see her getting fucked royally by you every second on my news feed, this bitch called my job and tried to get me fired. Good thing they love me at work, I was able to convince them that her claims were unsubstantiated."

The fact that she was jealous caught me off guard considering our situation with each other. I mean, she had seen me fuck other women with her own eyes, even rooted me on as I did it.

"Oh, and Truth is getting on my nerves too, telling me I'm buggin' for getting mad at that World Star video. Her little nasty ass been rubbing her pussy to it all day," Jasmine said with a snarl.

"Give me the phone!" Truth said.

"I'm not done."

"Give me the phone! Yo ass in your feelings because you on the rag, that's all!"

"Yo! King!"

"Yeah?" I said, with a smile, inching slowly towards a laugh because I knew she was about to say something ignorant.

"Yo! Word to Brooklyn, you fucked the shit out of that bitch!" She said laughing.

"I can't stand your ignorant ass sometimes!" Jasmine said, in the background.

"Go lay your ass down," Truth said, laughing.

"You see how she treats me, Travis?" Jasmine said, loud enough for me to hear.

"You coming by here tonight? I need to get fucked in the worst way after watching your video!"

"I thought you got off mad times already."

"I did! Shit, I'm still fucking horny."

"I don't know about today, I'm going to be too drained to give 100%."

"Ok, that's cool. You rest up because you're going to need every ounce of energy in your fucking body, I swear!!"

I laughed, "Hold up, I got an incoming call, let me call you back."

"Hello," I said.

"You're going to be sorry that you ignored me." Denise said.

"Aren't you about to get married?" I asked.

"I DON'T GIVE A FUCK!" she screamed, "DO NOT FUCKING IGNORE ME BITCH!"

"Bitch?" I replied.

When she started to scream again, I hung up while she was in mid-sentence. She called me three more times before leaving a message saying, "I HOPE THAT BITCH YOU FUCKING GOT A COMFORTABLE BED!!"

Yeah ok, this broad has officially lost it, I thought to myself. I turned up Jay-Z's "99 Problems" as I floored the gas pedal.

I loved my dates with Debbie and Anastasia; they got off on giving head. All they wanted me to do was sit there and get my knob polished as I talked shit to them, slapped their asses every now and then and fucked their throats until we all got off. Piece of cake. The only thing is, they didn't stop sucking until I busted three nuts, it's like a ritual. My third nut takes forever to come, and when it does, I'm so exhausted that I need a nap.

As they opened the door, they quickly hugged me, and then got down to business. Pulling me over to the love seat, Debbie pulled my pants, socks and shoes off, as Anastasia went right in, sucking my dick nice and slow until I was rock hard in her mouth.

Anastasia was tall and slim with a nice bubble ass, and a perky C-cup. She had a pouty mouth, slender nose and big, bedroom eyes."

"Lick those fucking balls bitch," I said, as I pushed Anastasia's head down. Immediately, Debbie started sucking my dick, stroking it with two hands. I grabbed her by her curly red hair, looking her in her eyes while she stroked my dick. I said, "Are you my little slut?" Nodding her head yes, I relinquished my grip as she went back to sucking it, going into a full on deep throat. "Sit up on the couch, both of you, so I can finger fuck your pussies." They both eased their wet pussies down on my middle and ring fingers. "That's right," I said, "I want pussy juice to drip all down my arms.

91

At this point, they were passing my dick back forth, taking turns gagging on it. Debbie was about 5'2, 160 lbs., thick! Huge rack, about a G- cup, nice waist line, and a big ol' ass that she took pride in. I began thrusting harder the wetter they got. They had been sucking my dick so long, they knew when I grew that extra inch or so I was about to cum. They started stroking it faster while flicking their tongues on my head. I shot my cum, a warm gooey load. At that instant, Anastasia came, nice and creamy. My dick was so jealous of my right hand's nut! Shortly after, Debbie came, like a fire hydrant! Explosive, pushing my hand out. The thought of them cumming on my dick instead of fingers got me right back.

Now they were starting at the base of my dick and licking all the way up to the tip. Once making it to passion's peak, they would French kiss with the head of my dick in between their mouths.

"That's right," I said, "Take your time with my dick. How does that dick taste, Bitch?" I slapped Anastasia's tight little ass

"It tastes good, daddy," she said, half mumbling with a mouthful of dick.

"How about you?" I said, as I shoved my dick further down Debbie's throat.

Gasping for air, she said, "It tastes like chocolate!"

I slid my fingers back inside them and they humped away. They were slapping each other's tongues with my big dick. Suddenly, I shot my load all over Debbie's face. My dick went numb. On cue like always, once I shot my load, they both shivered and gave my dick more reasons to be jealous. Lifting my left leg up, Debbie started to lick my ass and Anastasia began to suck my dick slow and deep. I could no longer talk shit anymore. I was speechless. My mouth wide open looking at Anastasia in her eyes as she took every inch of me into her beautiful mouth. I caressed her hair as she began to lick from my balls to my ass, back and forth.

"He's about to cum," Anastasia said, as they both began to rub their pussies ferociously, licking the head as I stood over them and stroked my big dick.

"Are my little slut's ready for this nut?"

"Yes sir," they said in unison.

Feeling the surge from my balls throughout my dick, I watched my cock spew up the last of its life. Long strings of cum everywhere, it felt as if I would never stop cumming. They came together as Debbie licked Anastasia's face clean, and then Anastasia returned the favor. Both of them smiling, looking at my dick was a sight to behold.

Driving up to my humble abode, the first thing I saw was police cars, fire trucks and all of my neighbors gathered around. A smell of ash and gasoline was in the air. From what I could make out, one of my neighbors seemed to have burned their place down. The closer I got, the more my perception of the situation changed. It wasn't one of the neighbors; the place being offered up for sacrifice was mine!

Throwing my car in park, I walked up slowly, watching my house burn helplessly as the flames devoured it, room by room. The fire chief in my left ear talking to me about insurance and the extent of the damage, my right ear being invaded by the whispers of gossip. I can almost guarantee none of these people were thinking about where I would lay my head tonight. I called Jasmine.

"Hey Travis!" Jasmine answered the phone in a far better mood then she was in earlier today.

"I'M GONNA KILL THAT BITCH!"

"What? WHO? Damn boy, what's wrong?"

"Denise burned my house down!"

"How do you know it was Denise that did it?"

"No one else had a motive. Either her, or Mike. Fuck it, I'm gonna kill him too" I said.

"Truth took the phone, "Where do you stay?"

"Take Chicago Ave to Austin, I stay across from Austin Street, where Oak Park begins."

"Say no more, we are on our way!"

As I sat in my car waiting for them to reach me. I began to think about how fake Mike has been these last couple of years as my best friend. I began to think about the lengths Denise was going to. I began to think about my profession, and how low I've sunk after the break up. Tear's started to well up in my eyes. I began wailing on my steering wheel. I beat and bashed on it until I was exhausted. Finally giving in, I rested my head on it taking a deep breath, closing my eyes, wishing that when I re-opened them I would awake from a dream.

Two raps at my window, I looked up to a concerned look on Jasmine's face. Straight ahead I could see Truth talking to the on-scene police and firemen. Jasmine opened my door reached in and gave me a tight embrace.

Taking my keys, she said, "Scoot over, Travis."

"Why? Where are we going?"

"We're going home," Jasmine said.

Rest Haven

That was some good ass sleep, I thought to myself. Waking up fully, I noticed Truth behind me with her hand around the base of my cock, as Jasmine slowly slid her pussy on my dick from the side. I played like I was asleep. Jasmine let out a loud moan.

"Girl, shut the fuck up! Hurry up, get that nut so we can switch," Truth whispered. Slowly, without being noticed, I pushed my pelvis out a bit, so she could get more of the dick. Feeling her tense up and then shiver, I said, "That will be five hundred dollars." Jasmine starting laughing.

Truth started snoring all of a sudden, slowly moving her hand from the base of my cock. "Your ass ain't asleep," I said, as I turned over to see Truth trying to hide a smile. Putting her legs around my waist, I eased into her, watching that smile turn into an expression of lust.

She bit her bottom lip and said, "Yesssssssss!"

As I stroked her, Jasmine took the tip of her extremely long tongue and began to toy with her love button. Truth began to cream on my dick. Jasmine commenced to

96

lapping it all up as she ran her tongue up my shaft and back down to Truth's enlarging clitoris.

"Oh my fucking god!" Truth said, as she began to tremble.

Pulling my dick out of her pussy just in time, I began to cum all over Jasmine's tongue. I fell back, ready to drift back to sleep, when Jasmine jumped on me trying to kiss me on my mouth, knowing I just jizzed on her tongue. After three unsuccessful attempts, she hops over on Truth who obliges her with a long passionate kiss.

It wasn't long until they gravitated back to me, Truth's head on the inside of my shoulder, Jasmine resting her head on my chest. *I can get used to this*, I thought to myself.

"Can we keep him?" Truth asked, with an innocent school girl look on her face.

"He ain't going anywhere," Jasmine said, with an air of confidence.

I will not be able to do that every day, considering my profession," I said trying to bring them back to reality. "Speaking of my profession, I have to get up and get to the mall, I literally have nothing."

"But this is how we want you, ass naked and confined to our bed," Truth said, as they both clamped hand cuffs around my wrist.

"No, for real, I got to be going. Thank you for hospitality but…"

At that moment, truth began to gag herself with my cock!

"Today is our off day, which means it's your off day too," Jasmine said, as she pulled my dick out of Truth's mouth and began to suck it passionately.

Off and on for the rest of the morning, they had their way with me. They released me near noon, but all I could do then was drift peacefully back to sleep.

Waking from a much needed slumber, I felt at peace, happy even. "Good evening, sleepy head," Jasmine said, with a mumble as she walked in the room brushing her teeth. "Here's the outfit we bought for you. We can all go shopping tomorrow, but tonight, we need to celebrate," she said, while doing an awful rendition of the cabbage patch.

"You're a fucking geek," Truth said, laughing then turning to me. Snatching the covers away, she said, "Get up, ya food is on the table. Take your stanky dick ass in the shower and wash up, then put on these clothes so we can get fucked up."

We all erupted with laughter.

"If my dick stinks it's because of that garbage truck juice y'all ass was spraying everywhere when I was dicking y'all down."

They both jumped me, playfully smacking my head and trying to tickle me.

I jumped out of the bed, "Aight, aight, I'll eat the meal you made for me. This is breaking news in Chicago. The first time ever in the history of the city two 'ratchet females' ghetto fabulously made breakfast for their well-endowed guest," I said with a chuckle.

"Ratchet?!" they said in unison. "Let's get his ass," Truth said, half laughing as she got up to chase me.

"So where are we headed out to?" I asked, as I buttoned up my cardigan.

"To the Fuck Me Harder hide out," Jasmine said.

"The girls miss you Travis," Truth said.

"Who? These girls?" I asked, as I playfully began to caress Truth's boobs.

"No, you freak!" she said laughing, "Our sisters from FMH."

"Shit, I miss them too," I said, the thought made my cock jump.

"Who is that doing the Adam's family knock at y'all door?" I asked.

"That's the weed man," Jasmine said.

"What's up, Boss Bitch? What's up First Lady?" Snow Flake said, as she walked in with the biggest bag of weed I had ever seen in my life.

"Hey, King," she said, as she hugged me tight.

Her ass was so big and round. She had dyed her hair and now had the Jennifer Aniston thing going on.

"I'm ready to suck someone's dick," Snow Flake said, as she looked me in my eyes.

"Make that two," Truth said, strap on in hand.

"The more, the merrier," Snow Flake said.

"You're such a fucking slut," Jasmine said, as she kissed Snow flake seductively.

"Travis, roll up," Truth said.

"I'm not much of a smoker, I can't roll," I said smiling.

"Rookie," she said.

"We got this. You just stand there and look good, seems you got that down pat."

After smoking what seemed to be an unlimited supply of marijuana, I was feeling good. A car horn blaring outside was starting to become a buzz kill.

"Quick that's the girls outside in the Limo! Somebody grab King, he's so fucked up," she said laughing.

I thought I was looking cool, but apparently I was struggling.

"I got him," Truth said.

She grabbed my arm and led me towards the door. Stopping just short of the door, she said, "Try to have a good time, Daddy. Forget about everything else, we got you."

"Keep your head up, both of them," she said, as she grabbed my dick and kissed me passionately.

As I stepped into the limo, I began to liven up. I saw the gang laughing, drinking and smoking. Make it Nasty was getting her pussy eaten already by Thick Wit It & Bodacious.

"Hey King," the girls said in Unison.

"Sit next to me," Boss Bitch said, while patting the seat next to her.

"Who ready to suck some dick?" Boss Bitch yelled out, as she poured me a glass of Ciroc.

All the girls began to chime up. While Boss bitch turned to kiss me some more, I noticed Jasmine and Super Soaker began to suck on Boss Bitch's strap on.

Boss Bitch began to unbuckle my belt, let's get this big ass dick out of its prison. Immediately, Snow Flake started to gag on it.

"You like that King? Does she do it better than me?" she asked, smiling.

I nodded my head yes.

"We'll see about that later," she said, planting another kiss on my lips.

"Aren't we going to close the window?" I said, looking at the driver taking peeks.

"Fuck 'em. Let him enjoy the show."

Watching Jasmine suck with so much passion was starting to make my dick harder. "I need some dick," Bodacious said, as she took Boss Bitches strap on out of Super Soaker's mouth and slid down on it, riding and tonguing Boss Bitch Down.

Jasmine and Super Soaker just commenced a 69 as if nothing even happened.

I noticed Co-Co secluded, watching the whole thing. I motioned her to me, taking her by the hand; I positioned her perfectly, my mouth making perfect use of her landing strip. As I probed her moist, pink pussy, I felt Snow Flake ease my big dick deep inside her tight, extremely wet pussy. She began saying, "Oh my gosh!" over and over until finally I was filling her spot up to the hilt.

I had to use two hands to hold up Co-Co's super thick ass. Her pussy was quenching my thirst better than any watermelon had done before. I began to slurp on her hardening clit.

"Look at that white bitch take all of that black dick," Bodacious said between moans. The rest of the girls were cheering her on as she came over and over down the shaft of my iron hard dick. Before I could tell Snow Flake I was about to cum, she was already gagging on my dick, letting the cum ooze out of her mouth, onto her huge breasts.

Co-Co began to break her silence, she held my head in place as she creamed all in my mouth. Her taste was so sweet. Maybe I was tripping but she tasted like mangos!

"Looks like we are here," First Lady said.

One by one, I took the hand of each lady, helping them out of the limo. They were stunning; one could never imagine that they were all stone cold freaks behind closed doors.

"What the FUCK!?"

I snatched my hand back. Instead of Truth sticking out her hand for me to help her, she extended her dildo.

"You play too much," I said laughing, as I helped her out of the limo.

"Only when I'm around you," she said, as she gave me a soft kiss on the lips.

Turning around to tip the driver, he stopped me, handing me an envelope. "The pleasure was all mine," he said with a slight smile. Confused, I walked off, joining Truth and the girls.

"Truth, look." I showed her the now open envelope full of one hundred dollar bills.

She smiled, "Expect a lot of that tonight."

"Why," I asked?

"Let's just say FMH has a lot of admirers willing to pay to watch us in action."

Jasmine chimed in, "They also are willing to pay Truth top dollar to train a lot of their pets." By pets she meant their subs. "Oh, and the driver, he owns this place, in case you were wondering where the money came from."

This train was moving extremely fast, but I was loving every minute of it.

Level Ten

The scene was a lot different throughout the mansion. There still were the onlookers gazing in on their favorite genre of live porn. However, now there was sex happening throughout the whole mansion. On the stairs, in the lobby, throughout every corridor, in the bathrooms. It was like a buffet of lust. The veil that shielded us from the outsiders was now removed. I was so worked up; I just had to have the taste of a moist, tantalizing, delicious pussy in my mouth. "I want all you to lean back and spread your fucking legs. Take your favorite toy and get those pussies nice and wet for me."

"First Lady, you're going to help me lick all of these pussies into submission." Starting with Bodacious, we began to take turns kissing her pussy softly, gradually building up intensity gradually. As I French kissed her clit, Jasmine began to slide her tongue deep into her pussy.

"Ohhhhh shiiitttt! Stay right fucking there!" Bodacious said as she pushed my face deeper into her crotch. Jasmine began to kiss me between long strokes of her tongue starting from the bottom of Bodacious' pussy, to her now hardened clit. Drunk with lust, I decided that every one of my ladies will feel my tongue deep in their asses tonight. The ladies were enjoying the show as well, I could hear their moans intensify, getting louder as the seconds went by. My tongue sliding deep into her ass pushed her over the edge. She went into one of the most powerful orgasms I have ever seen. I grew so hard from watching her cum. I just wanted to fuck the living shit out of her. However, I would not be derailed from my goal. I wanted to make it known that I was willing to do whatever it took to keep my girls satisfied. Jasmine and I made it all the way around the room, out of breath, faces wet from the facial abuse we just took, and we began to make out. Jasmine started to lick my lips clean as she stroked my dick.

"Look at all of these people we have turned on," I looked around slowly seeing women and men masturbating, making out, even having sex while watching us.

I turned Jasmine around so we were looking directly at the onlookers. I began to stroke her puss from the side, pulling my dick out after every long stroke teasing her. I felt a sense of pride as Jasmine frantically reached for my cock whenever I wasn't inside of her, as if our physical connection was mandatory, like breathing air. I focused my eyes on a very attractive Hispanic woman in the crowd of onlookers. With my hand around Jasmine's throat, I began to pound her pussy harder. I noticed my admirer biting her bottom lip. She tugged on her sub's leash, a white male, looking around thirty five years old, average build. She began to fuck his face while looking into my eyes. Jasmine began to cry out in pleasure!

"FUCK ME HARDER BABY! YES, FUCK ME LIKE THE LITTLE SLUT THAT I AM!"

Not taking my eyes off my admirer, I began to caress, and then lightly slap Jasmine's face just like she loves it. She began to come all over my dick. I kept fucking her without mercy, eyes on my admirer. As she came all over her pets face, I pulled out and shot my load, covering Jasmine's whole left butt cheek. Make It Nasty came over and licked up all of my cum. Watching her enjoy the taste of my seed made my dick rise again. Looking around I saw Boss Bitch slapping Thick Wit It's big juicy ass with a paddle, while having her tied up and suspended in the air. I began to kiss Thick Wit It's soft, full lips. For a moment I wished she wasn't blind folded that way I could stare into her eyes as I inserted my big throbbing erection deep into her pussy. "Damn boy, I missed that big fucking dick," she said as I filled her to the hilt. Putting her finger to her lips, Boss Bitch slid her strap-on into Thick Wit It's big, smooth, perfectly round ass.

"Oh my fucking god, yesss!!" she purred.

We began to stroke her deep, in unison.

"That's right, fuck me like you own this pussy," Thick Wit It pleaded.

Jasmine joined us, holding me from the back.

Looking me in my eyes, Boss Bitch whispered, "I love you."

Jasmine kissed my ear lobe and said, "We love you."

"I love you too," I said as I began to fuck Thick Wit It more passionately.

"SHUT THE FUCK UP BITCH AND TAKE THIS DICK!" Boss Bitch said as she covered Thick Wit It's mouth, as we both plowed away at her wet gaping holes.

"I'm about to cum," I said.

"Don't you fucking stop! Fill the pussy up with your cum," Boss Bitch said.

"That's what you like right?" Jasmine said knowing Thick Wit It and I both had a cream pie fetish.

"Come in my fucking pussy, Daddy, please! Quench my thirst," Thick Wit screamed.

I began to spill me seed deep into her pussy.

"Yes, oohhhh shit! Yes!" My coming lead to her squirting every fucking where. Taking the blindfold off of Thick Wit It, her eyes said, "thank you," as her mouth said, "That was interesting!" We all chuckled.

Boss Bitch and I DP'd the whole gang! We had to actually mop the floor after fucking Super Soaker. She gave the term "make it rain" a whole new meaning.

After the show was over, the spectators gave quiet applause and began to file out, leaving white envelopes at the table by the door. "You don't have to share our dick with strangers no more," Make It Nasty said. "Super Soaker and I were propositioned by Mr. Friendly, the owner, so we came up with this idea."

"The onlookers are all movers and shakers that Mr. Friendly knows from his corporate and political circles."

"I suggest you mingle a bit, I hear there are a few writer's out there," Jasmine said.

"Yeah, I might as well," I said.

So we all got dressed, went out and enjoyed the party as if nothing ever happened.

Un-Charted Waters

Moving in with Jasmine and Truth had turned out to be a good choice. I didn't think I'd like it at first, being that I've been a single bachelor for so long.

Truth came in, slamming the door, "LOOK AT MY FUCKING FACE!" she said.

"Who the fuck did this to you?" I jumped up to get better view. "A perp," she said, "We got a domestic disturbance call from dispatch that just so happened to share the same address as a dope spot we been staking out. The situation got out of hand, the initial on-scene responders drew down on the guy. I got in there to try to diffuse the situation and the bastard socked me right in my fucking eye."

"Got damn," I said, "It's just a little mouse though, it will be gone in a week's time with pressure and a cold pack."

"Poor baby!" Jasmine said, coming in the front room with ice wrapped in a towel.

"Look at you though, jumping up getting all protective over me, that shit got me excited," Truth said.

"Don't get too excited, you not getting no dick with your face looking like that!" I said playfully.

"Boy please, in fact get over here and suck on this pussy! You too bitch," she said while grabbing Jasmine by the hair. Snatching her jeans off, then ripping off her panties, I began to lick her clit in circles as Jasmine joined me.

"FUCK YES. THAT'S RIGHT!! EAT MY FUCKING PUSSY, MMMMMMMMM!"

I began to pull down Jasmine's boy shorts, easing my rock hard erection, into her dripping wet pussy. I was in heaven. We began to French kiss with Truths clit in the middle. "That big dick is filling that pussy up huh?" Truth asked.

"Save some of that dick for me baby.   I want you to nut all in this pussy too, Daddy."

Watching Jasmine's eyes roll into the back of her head just made my dick grow longer and thicker. Jasmine began to tongue fuck Truth's pussy just how I was fucking her pussy, slow and deep.

Truth sat up on her elbows so she could get a better view of us both lapping at her clit like two thirsty kittens lapping water on a hot summer day.

"Suck that clit you sexy motherfucker," Truth said. As she pushed my head further, squirting in both of our faces, she still managed to talk shit.

I shot a load into Jasmine, but my dick was still hard as concrete. I kept stroking her. Her big ass bouncing all over my long, thick dick.

"I love this fucking dick," she said between mouthfuls of pussy.

"Shut the fuck up, bitch, and tongue fuck that pussy. The only sound I should hear is y'all suckin' on this pussy, and that big dick destroying your pussy. Ohhh Fuck! I'm about to come baby! Ohhh Fuck! Oh shiittttttttt!" she said half crying.

Jasmine began to lick her pussy with the speed of light.

I started to fuck Jasmine harder as I threw her back on my dick by her shoulders.

All of us coming together was a sound that was so beautiful, the scene was so intense it was like an out-of-body experience. Like I was there watching myself with two of the most beautiful women ever created, having my way with them.

Staring at Truth, I abruptly pulled my still raging hard dick from Jasmine's cunt, and started to fuck Truth's throat. She was in heaven. As much as she loved barking orders, she loved being man-handled more. My left hand on her head with my leg up, I forced all the dick down her throat while palming Jasmine's ass telling her how good her pussy felt to me.

Truth pulled my dick out of her mouth and spit on it, stroking it slowly then fucking her beautiful face with it. I couldn't take it anymore; pulling her off her knees I threw her on the couch and began to fuck her missionary as hard as I could.

"Jasmine get over here and fuck her face with that pretty little pussy of yours."

I began to slap Jasmine's big, juicy ass, then kissing her cheeks, as I pounded away at Truth's tight pussy. Grabbing my head, Jasmine pushed my face further into her ass cheeks. I began to lick her asshole with reckless abandon.

"I'm cumming, Daddy! Baby, suck that pussy just.... like... that!"

I began to cum deep inside of Truth's pussy as she creamed on my dick. She pulled me in tighter as if she wanted all of my cum inside of her.

The thought of it pushed me into a multiple-orgasm. Load after load splashed against the walls of her pussy. I laid inside her while kissing them both.

Jasmine was looking at Truth for an extended period of time, then at me, and asked,

"What do you think of polygamy?"

Truth perked up to hear my answer.

"I never really thought about it. I can imagine it's a lot of responsibility. It's hard enough to provide for and understand one woman, let alone multiple."

"What if you didn't have to provide for them?" Truth said.

"I'm a man though; I have to be the provider."

"What if you and your partners worked as a team when it came to monetary issues?" Jasmine said.

"That would be a big release of pressure. However, the understanding of multiple women, their emotions, mood swings…is too much for me. I hate drama."

"What if that was handled as a collective unit as well?" Jasmine said.

"I don't want to be married though, titles complicate everything," I said.

"Neither do we," they both said.

"Travis, we want to try this with you. When I say we, I mean all of the girls. Your sexual appetite is big enough for all of us. You're loving, protective, gentle, but firm when you have to be."

Cutting Jasmine off, Truth said, "Plus, you're fine as hell and fuck the shit out of us."

I started to laugh. "Y'all serious?"

"As a heart attack," Jasmine said.

"We all want children soon.   Our biological clocks are ticking, and we don't want a donor. We want to share these experiences with each other," Jasmine said.

"Speaking of that, you're about to be a father in about seven months!" Truth blurted out.

"HUH!?! Come again?"

"April is two months pregnant," she said smiling. "We are happy but a little jealous too! Especially her," Jasmine said while pointing at Truth.

I was still trying to do math in my head. Two months ago at our first show, Truth and myself had her tied up and fucked her good.

It was a definite possibility. "Why didn't she tell me?"

"She wanted to know your position on this topic first."

"So all y'all trying to get pregnant in succession?"

"No, most of the sister's still got traveling and other things they want to knock out first, so they will remain on birth control," Jasmine said.

"But I do, so I hope he's ready," she said patting my semi-hard cock.

"Let's see where this goes," I said optimistically.

They both smiled and hugged me.

"Let's call the girl's over for a sleepover," Jasmine said.

"Shouldn't we call it a fuckover? We all know no one will be getting any sleep tonight."

Sitting on the loveseat, getting my dick sucked slowly by Jasmine while watching Truth fuck herself with her eight inch long, thick ass dildo, one by one the girls started coming in.

Without saying a word, they just joined in the party. Monica, aka Make it Nasty, went right over to Boss Bitch and took over sliding the dildo in and out, slurping on her clit. Super Soaker, aka Trina, gave me a nice passionate kiss, then went and planted her fat pussy right on Boss Bitch's face. Co-Co, aka Sarah, came up right next to me and began to play with her sweet pussy. Snow Flake, aka Fran, got on her knees and began to gag on my big dick, alternating turns with Jasmine.

Thick Wit It, aka April, came in with Bodacious, "There goes my Baby Daddy," she said, kissing me, then plopping her pretty pussy on my face. Bodacious, aka Jane sat her pussy on Sarah's face. "Get this pussy nice and wet for him to nut all in. This good pussy," she told Sarah.

Looking down at my dick, it was bigger and harder than I've ever seen it. Jasmine and Fran knelt there in awe of their handy work. "Come here, bitch, and take all of this nut in your pussy," Fran said, as she held the base of my dick. Sliding her luscious frame down on my dick, I began to kiss her passionately as we began to grind slowly. "You are a sexy bitch, aren't you?" I asked.

"I'm *your* sexy bitch, Daddy," she purred in my ear.

I began to fuck her deeper.

"YES, FUCK ME HARDER DADDY, BEAT THAT PUSSY INTO SUBMISSION!"

With my left hand holding her hands behind her back, I began to choke her with my right, slamming her big ass down on my dick.

"Suck on my fucking tongue," I said as I punished her pussy for being so good.

"Where you want me to cum?" I asked.

"In my pussy..."

"Where?" I asked again as I slapped her ass.

"In my pussy, Daddy," she said as she came all over my dick.

I spread her ass cheeks pushing my dick in as deep as I could go and began unloading my seed.

"That's what the fuck I'm talking about. Mmmmmm, cum all in that pussy! Ohhhhh shit, give me all that fucking nut."

"Save some for me," Fran said between moans as Jasmine was probing her cunt with her long ass tongue.

Pulling my dick out of her pussy, Bodacious began to suck it slow and passionate, "Fran you ready girl? This is one big ass slab of meat!" she said.

"I was born ready for that big dick," she said as she slid it deep into her pussy.

I began to slap her big white ass, hard as I could, caressed the spot I slapped then smacked it again.

"That's what she need, Daddy. She's been a bad little whore," Co-Co said as she started to rub her pussy even faster. I love the fact that Co-Co loved to masturbate; she looked so good doing it. "Come here, Co-Co," I said as I stroked Snow Flake's pussy into frenzy.

"Keep rubbing your pussy, I just want to kiss you," I said. I began to kiss her passionately. Then Fran began to kiss her, it became a contest to see who could make her pussy drip more. Fran's pussy was so wet and warm. Co-co looked me in my eyes and said, "Nut in that pussy, Daddy, so I can lick it out." I began to fuck Fran harder.

"Yes, give me that big, black, beautiful dick! Fuck me, Fuck me, Fuck me!!"

"Give me that cum," she began to whisper in my ear, over and over. As I began to cum her eyes rolled to the back of her head. She slid off my still rigid dick.   Co-Co began to lick her now red pussy, I slid my big dick into Co-Co doggy style and pushed her face deeper into Fran's Pussy. I began to pulverize Co-Co's pussy while watching Jasmine and Boss Bitch have a pussy-eating contest. Boss Bitch was devouring Make it Nasty's pussy, while Jasmine was taking wave after wave of Super Soaker's juices.

I had Co-Co by the neck fucking her like there was no tomorrow, while Fran slipped her tongue in Co-Co's mouth.

"I'm trying to do your dick like I'm doing her face," Super Soaker said in between powerful orgasms.

"Daddy, I want that nut all in my fucking mouth and on my titties, Daddy," she said as she began to suck her own breast. I grabbed her by both of her elbows and began to wail on her pussy walls. "This pussy is so fucking good," I whispered in her ear. She began to cream all over my dick. I felt the urge to cum so I pulled my dick out and began to stroke it nice and slow in Co-Co's face.

"That fucking cock is huge," Fran said as she nibbled on Co-Co's ear. Looking Fran right in the eyes as I stroked my big dick, watching her begin to rub herself, I begin to tense up feeling my nut about to come. I erupt all over Co-Co's face and tits.

"Ohhhh Shit, Daddy. Damn that's a lot of fucking cum."

"That could have been in you, but you choose otherwise," I said to laughter, quoting Martin Lawrence from one of his stand-ups.

We continued to fuck off and on between naps until the sun came up.

Mystery Woman

Some people hate jogging in the rain, but I love it. I love breathing in the air during a good rain. Also running against the wind builds your endurance. *I'll take a detour through these woods; I never ran this trail, let me see what it's all about.*

"So do you run this trail often?" The voice was definitely a Latin woman.

I turned to see my admirer from our first performance.

"It's my first time. How about you?"

"I run this trail every day at this time."

"Nice," I said. "My name is Marks, Trav Marks."

"Mines is Maria."

"Nice, like the Virgin Mary," I said.

"Nothing like her," she said with a sly smile.

"Why is that?" I asked.

"If you knew what I was thinking you wouldn't ask," she said.

"Well why don't you tell me?" I was growing intrigued.

Her snug jogging suit hugged her slim waist and big hips perfectly.   I began to grow stiff.

"I'm thinking about you pounding my big, Latina ass with your huge cock."

"Where?" I asked.

"Right here, behind that tree," she said.

Pulling out my dick, she gagged on it a couple of times getting it nice and wet. "It's so much bigger in person. Damn!"

"Hurry, Papi. Get that dick in there," she said as she pulled down her jogging pants revealing a huge firm ass. I eased my dick in inch by inch. She stared at me the same way she did at the show.

"I have two subs at home that love to watch; maybe you can have your way with me in front of them. I'll make sure you are compensated," she said between moans.

"Maybe I will," I said as I was finally able to get my whole cock inside of her. "But for now I need you to shut the fuck up and take this dick."

 I covered her mouth, grabbed a hand full of hair, and began to dig her deep. Her ass was so tight and wet. I moved my hand to kiss her soft lips.

"Your dick is so fucking good. I wish you can fuck me like this for an eternity."

I began to bite and suck her neck, as I fucked her nice and steady. Her long thick legs, were toned, she stood their taking every inch of me like a stallion.

"Choke me, and fuck me harder." she pleaded. I began to speed up, telling her how good she felt on my dick. She would rub her pussy extremely fast whenever she was about to cum.

"I want to be your dirty little cock whore," she said as she stared into my eyes.

I began to come deep in her ass. I kept stroking.

"My God, your dick just got harder," she said as she bit her lip. "Fuck my face. Abuse my fucking throat," she said as she squatted down, taking my dick to the back of her throat.

I began to fuck her mouth hard and fast, her tears made her mascara run down her face. She pulled my cock out of her mouth, long enough to spit on it. Stroking it slowly, she asked, "Can I please have this big dick in my pussy, Sir?"

"How bad do you want it in your pussy?"

"Really bad, Sir."

"Show me how bad?"

She took my cock in her mouth, sucking slowly and passionately, then abruptly fucking her face with it, alternating back and forth between the two forms of pleasure. I pulled her up by her hair. I began smacking her big ass, then I slid my big dick in her Latin pussy and began to fuck her soul. She began to talk Spanish to me as I pummeled her tight little pussy.

"You're my little whore?"

"Yes sir. I love your fucking big cock. Please don't stop fucking me."

I wanted to cum in her badly. I started to think about the girls and recanted. I slid my dick back into her asshole and began to fuck her into submission.

"YES!! Fuck yes!" she screamed.

As I began to fill her ass up with yet another huge load of my warm cum, she fell back into me. I held her tight until she could regain her composure.

"You're amazing," she said.

"So are you."

Tying her hair back into a pony tail she asked, "So, do we have a deal? "Once a month we meet up, you fuck the shit out of me and we go our separate ways."

"Sounds good to me," I said with a smile.

She kissed my cheek as she slipped me her business card. I took it even though I had no intention of calling her. I didn't want to make a spectacle.

As she jogged off I thought to myself "What the fuck did I just do?" I had a tinge of guilt descend upon me suddenly like a bald eagle snatching its prey out of the river's end. I quickly cast it aside, instead thinking about how I need to take the girls out. *We'll go shopping first, dinner, then a movie. I'll have to take care of Co-Co and Jasmine when they get back in town.*

Home Alone

Chilling at home with Truth was like being at the crib with one of the fellas.

"Trav, you trying to get your ass bust on this NBA2K?" Truth asked.

"Nah, Babe. I'm working on my book right now."

"Speaking of your book, that shit is HOT! I read a chapter and it had my pussy leaking!"

126

"For real though?" I asked as I laughed.

"Hell yeah. I know shit about us is true, but how much of that other shit is true?"

"All of it," I said.

"All of it? She paused the game and looked at me."

"All of it," I repeated.

"You a bad muthafucka," she said laughing. "AND yo' ass been holding out!"

"How so?"

"Shit, I want you to massage me with oils, and fuck me in the candlelight all slow and passionate like you did that bitch in yo' book," she said laughing but serious.

"I didn't think you would be into that though."

"Why the fuck not?" she asked, shrugging and talking with her hands and shoulders like a true New Yorker.

"Because you so tomboy-ish.   I figured I had to lay it down rough so you knew what time it was."

"True. I love how you be slinging it to me, but still, after reading that shit, I need that."

"You sound crazy right now saying that shit with those Timbs, fitted jeans, and that Yankee fitted though!"

"Fuck you, Babe," she said laughing.

I continued to write away trying to break through this writer's block I was experiencing.

"Babe, look," she said.

I looked up to see her standing their naked. Flawless. Her tight body, perfect -sized breasts, and nice, round, bubble butt.

"Can I get a fucking massage now?" she asked.

I smiled. Looking back down at my laptop screen, which was still blank after an hour, I thought *Why not?*

Carrying her to the room, I noticed her body was tense. Not because she thought I would mishandle her. She was not accustomed to relinquishing this type of control.

"Relax, I got you," I whispered.

"You got me?" she repeated softly, almost childlike.

"I got you," I reiterated while kissing her forehead.

I lie her softly on the bed, laying kisses on her from her head down to her feet. Rubbing my hands together for warmth, then pouring a small amount of massage lotion on them, I began to rub her feet with a nice firm grip.

"That feels really, really good," she purred.

I moved up to her thighs, while kissing the back of her left knee, I made sure to rub her inner thigh, getting as close to her pretty, neatly-trimmed pussy as possible without actually touching it. She began to embrace my touch, my hands and her body in perfect harmony. I turn her over, taking her right leg and starting the process over from the top. I place a sensual kiss, on her clit. She grabbed my head, trying to push me further, but I resisted. Kissing up her toned stomach, adding more oil, I began to massage her breasts. Taking one at a time, I diligently sought to please every inch of her wonderfully built set.

"I want you inside of me," she said.

"Not yet. I need you to turn over, Baby," I responded as our lips locked, instigating the battle between lust and love, the never-ending struggle with passion.

I started to work on her shoulders, alternating between a firm grip and light, caressing touch, placing my thumbs, letting my hands fall naturally to either side of her now very willing body. I run my thumbs along her spine down to her lower back. My manhood grew so hard it began to ache. Pulsating, it's only remedy was the slice of heaven that lay wait between her thighs. I went back to her spine.

"I love you so much," I whispered in her ear.

Kissing down her back allowed me to slide off my boxer briefs unaware. I kiss her cheeks, biting and sucking softly on each of them.   She began to melt under each kiss. I go back to kissing her spine, this time sliding my raging hard cock deep inside of her as I bit and sucked her neck.

"Baby, your dick feels so hard in my pussy," she said as reached back to grab my head. Slow, steady strokes each hitting the same spot. Wave after wave of her love, splashed against my cock.

"I fucking love you, Travis!" she cried out trembling in the midst of an orgasm.   Still I stroked her slow and steady.

Wrapping my arms around her in a tight embrace, I stroked deeper. I became lost deep inside her world. So deep that when I began to release, it pained me as much as it pleasured me. A beautiful yet torturing experience. We laid there, both trembling, connected mind, body, and spirit, descending back down to earth.

After a brief silence. I decided that I must tell her the truth. NO MORE HIDING!

"Travis, I have to tell you something that's very important."

"I have to tell you something too," I said.

"Ok, you go first," she said.

Taking a deep breath, I began to speak but nothing came out. I put the ball back in her court.   "Nah, you got first," I said nervously laughing.

"How about we both go on the count of three," she said.

"Ok, cool."

One.

Two.

Three.

"I cheated!" we both said in unison.

An awkward silence fell over us. Even though I did what I did, I felt betrayed. Wondering, *Was he better than me? Did he look better than me? Was he successful? Did she love him?* I had a lot of questions; I just couldn't bare the truth they may reveal.

"WHO THE FUCK IS SHE?" Truth belted out.

"You know the Latin chick, with the two pets?" I said looking at her from peripheral vision.

"Get the fuck out of here," she said laughing hysterically. I thought to myself, *what in the hell could she find funny about this?*

"Nigga, when was this?"

"Today, while I was out on my run, in the woods."

She laughed harder!

"What the fuck is so funny?" I said growing perturbed.

"I fuck that bitch too!" she said. We both started laughing.

"Man get the fuck outta here!" I said in tears.

"I went to her house and slayed her, while her pets were watching."

"We need fucking help," I said.

"No you the one that needs help, fucking in the woods and shit!" she said laughing so hard she snorted.

"What do we do about the girls? Should we tell them?" I asked.

Looking at each other for a split second, "HELL NO!" we said in unison.

Embracing each other again, Truth said, "We got a lot of shopping and ass-kissing to do."

"I was thinking the same exact thing," I said smiling.

Truth and I grew a bond that was peculiar for a man and woman to have. She had taken the place of Mike. I could talk to her about manly things without getting the built in cliché rebuttal responses some women use to deflect unfavorable situations. Allowing Truth to be who she naturally is has taken my bond with the rest of the girl's to another level. What they are not willing to tell me, she is. She's an untamed freak, with a soft side on one hand. And she's my boy on the other hand. Which is something that I had to get used to, I'm really protective of my manhood. I didn't particularity like Truth stepping in on my duties. It took Jasmine having a sit down with me to open my eyes.

"Travis, I assure you Truth is not trying to phase you out," she said smiling.

"Then why is she always veering into my lane?" I asked.

"Because that is the only lane she knows. She has always been the dominant one in all of her relationships. She has never dealt with a man before on this level. I'm in awe every time I look at the two of you interacting. Whether we all are playing board games, or fucking like it's no tomorrow, the love and respect in her eyes for you is crazy. She loves your masculinity, she is not intimidated by it, and her duplication of it is mere flattery. Just look how she melts in your hands when you kiss her. She loves you,

Travis. She just loves you in a different way. In such a way that sometimes the rest of the girl's, even myself, are envious of," she said with a laugh.

"Why envious I asked?"

"Y'all have this androgynous connection," she laughed.   I joined her.

"Androgynous? Ok that's a first."

"Yes, just think about it. Compared to the average man, your knowledge of women, what makes them tick, fashion… even your gossiping capabilities are uncanny!"

"Gossip?" I asked with my face twisted up. "Since when do I gossip?"

"You may not have noticed you gossip, Travis, but the girl's and I have gotten you going on a couple of topics," she said laughing. It doesn't make you less than a man, Babe," she said smiling while making an attempt to kiss the smirk off my face.

"For those simple moments we are glad that you aren't too manly to shop with us, go to the spa, sit in the salon and chime in on celebrity gossip while waiting on us to get our hair done. However, out of all us, Truth is the only one that reciprocates that naturally. We may go to a game with you, but she loves being there. We may sit in the barbershop with you, but not only is she there she's playing the dozen's with the barbers, and she gets a dap by everybody on the way out. You are in touch with your feminine side, and she is a tomboy. The synergy between you, all of the rest of my girls and myself help us enjoy this family we've created. So don't get upset with her. You have a lot of prissy, spoiled divas on your hands, we are not easy to handle. As much as you think she is in your lane, you are in hers too and it's perfect."

After that talk I saw Truth in a whole new light.

"So you know how this whole week has been about Monica and Trina considering they share same birthday?" Truth asked.

"Yeah between the two of them a brother about to go broke," I said with a chuckle.

"Well they just texted me from the room we booked for them, they want something else."

"Man, hell no," I said laughing but serious.

"Just look at the text," she said.

After reading the text, I spit my drink out across the bar. The bartender gave me the evil eye, she was not amused. "I apologize," I pleaded as I increased her tip.

Truth sat there, watching my every movement, waiting on an answer.

"Alright I will do it. Only because I love their asses," I said.

"Oh, this is going to be good," Truth said as she ordered two more shots of tequila.

"Hey ladies, look what the wind blew in," Truth said as she lead me into the suite by leash and collar as the ladies requested. They laid next to one another at the edge of the bed legs spread rubbing their clitoris.

"Bring him over here, he looks a little thirsty," Super Soaker said grabbing the leash from Truth with one hand, and pushing my face into her pussy with the other.

I began to eat her as if my life depended on it. I slid my middle and ring fingers into Monica, as I devoured Trina's pussy.

"That's right, eat that pussy make it squirt! Eat that shit just like that."   She palmed the back of my head and began to fuck my face. Monica was creaming all over my fingers.

"The girls are going to love this shit!" Truth said as she filmed everything.

"That's right, stay right there baby, I'm about to…OHHHHH FUCKKKKK!" she released her passion.

"Come here motherfucker," she said as she pulled me up by my leash. Kissing me with her full lips, licking my face clean as she held me by the chin she asked, "I bet you want to stick your cock in me, don't you? DON'T YOU?"

I nodded my head 'yes.'

"Not a fucking chance. Gets the fuck over there. Eat her pussy until she cums like a good little boy. Let's put those big juicy lips of yours to use," she said as she began to ride my face in the cowgirl position.

My dick was so hard it could have been used as a diving board. I could hear, Monica and Trina tongue-wrestling as my face was brutally pummeled by her sweet, wet, and willing pussy. Trina taking the torture to a whole other level began to ride just the tip of my dick. Laughing, she said, "I hope you didn't plan on getting a nut tonight."

Monica's body began to tense up and shiver. She let out a long, slow moan, and then collapsed next to me. We continued on this path until the girls were exhausted from so many orgasms.

Removing the collar and leash from my neck, Trina kissed my lips saying, "Thank you, Travis. You made my night."

Giving me a tight embrace, Monica said, "You were awesome! I don't think I ever came that much."

"Let's get you home," Truth said.

Starting up the engine, I pulled out my dick and said "Look at this shit! I'm definitely going to have blue balls in the morning," while laughing.

"Not on my watch. Shut up and drive while I work on releasing all this tension in this big fucking cock," Truth said as she took me in her mouth slowly.

I pulled out of the hotel parking lot feeling like royalty.

Fighting Temptation

Listening to the many voicemails left by my clients was driving me insane. I couldn't lie, I really missed fucking every last one of them. As happy as I am, I still had these cravings.

"So what lead to you enter the escort business?" Fran asked while she pulled her blond hair behind her ears to keep it from blowing in the wind. I began to answer but my phone interrupted me in mid-sentence.

"Hey."

"Hello, Baby.   I got bad news."

"What's that?" I said. My mind automatically starting to think about the baby.

"The baby is fine.   He's growing stronger and stronger daily."

"What a minute. Did you just say he?"

"Yes, it's going to be a boy!!" she said smiling through the phone.   I smiled.   Looking over at Fran I noticed she was smiling too.

"We love and miss you," Fran, said loud enough for April to hear.

"Awww," April said. "I missed y'all as well, but I'm not going to make it tonight."

"Why not?" I asked.

"My flight out of DC has been canceled.   I'm on my way back to my mother's right now."

"Damn, that sucks. So when will you be heading back out this way, April?"

"First thing in the morning.   I can't wait either. I'm so fucking horny," she whispered into the phone.

"Aren't you always," I said playfully.

"Not like this. But anyways, I'm not going to hold you. Drive safely, Travis.   Bye, Fran."

"Talk to you later," Fran said with a big smile.

"She's such an angel," Fran said with her Louisiana accent.

"Yeah, she is, I said reflecting on her for a moment. Yeah, I was saying, after my initial break up with Denise, my life went to shambles. I wasn't writing.   I ended up going from one dead end job to another. I was drinking heavy every day. I was a mess. After maybe three months of sulking, I picked myself up, got a good shower, shave and headed towards the beach to see if I could get some writing in. I ran into Mary Ann, a tall, slim, sexy brunette who owned her own escort service. After exchanging wits, she asked me if I'd be interested. I obliged and the rest is history."

"So how did you get into business for yourself?"

"I got fired," I said laughing. "Mary Ann and I started screwing something serious.   When I told her I wasn't ready for a relationship, she fired me. Luckily for me, when I met clients, I would give them my personal number as well. After a weeks' time, they began to call my personal phone to book appointments. Word of mouth spread and my business took off."

"Thinking of you having so many women crave you is turning me on. I need to be tied up and fucked like the dirty little whore that I am. Can you do that for me?" she asked as we pulled up to her place.

It was warm and cozy, pictures of us spaced out everywhere. She was not shy about our polygamous set up. "I've had this for years, waiting on the right man to experience it with," she said as she handed me the rope.

"Get out those fucking clothes."

"Yes, Sir," she said as she undressed quickly.

I kissed her slowly with devious intent, and then placed duct tape across her mouth. Tying her hands and feet snuggly, I placed her knees closer to her chest, pulling her bottom to the edge of the bed. I begin to caress her ass, giving it a nice, unexpected slap that sent chills down her spine.

I took her paddle, and began to give her steady slaps across both ass cheeks. Not too hard, not to soft but firm. At this point she was soaking wet. I took my cock and teased her, sliding it in all the way. She shook, nodded her head 'yes'. I held it there, then abruptly snatched it out, replacing it with my tongue. She began to wiggle and squirm, she was trying to communicate with me so I pulled off the tape.

"I want that dick inside of me," she said while panting.

Looking her in her eyes as I kissed her, I asked, "How bad?"

"Really bad."

"Are you lying?"

"No, Sir."

I grabbed a handful of her hair and began to fuck her throat as I placed what looked like the largest vibrator in the world on her clit. She began to moan louder.

"Open your mouth wider," I said as I fucked her throat until she gagged. Meanwhile a sea of pleasure shot out of her every five minutes. I pulled my cock out of her mouth and rammed it into her wet snatch as she lay there bound. My right hand pulling her hair, my left gripping her waist, I began to pound away, barking command after command. I shot load after load inside of her until my cock went limp. I fell exhausted beside her.

I began to undo the rope; she turned around to look at me and said "I think I owe you some money after that fucking performance!"

We both started to laugh.

"We need to hurry back, the girls was talking about a spades tournament."

"What the hell YOU know about spades?" I asked while smiling.

"Man, please sleep on a white girl if you want to, I have skills."

"Yes, you do indeed," I said looking her up and down.

"Haven't you had enough?   You got off like four nuts, and I counted."

"One could never have enough," I said as I pushed her legs back, pushing me all the way inside of her until her eyes rolled back.

"Just one more nut," I said before we began another journey to ecstasy.

Big Surprises in Small Packages

Last night was a fucking blast. We celebrated my poetry book debut all night! TEN THOUSAND books sold in the first week! I'm no Maya Angelou, but I can live with that. We drank, danced, laughed and I kicked their asses in spades. *They can't fuck with me*, I thought as I woke up stretching and yawning. Only Jasmine remained, everybody else must have gotten up to meet April at the airport. I threw on a pair of basketball shorts and a tank top to check the mail. As I reached for the door, Jasmine said, "I wouldn't do that if I was you."

"Why not?" I said, turning around to look at Jasmine. Then the bottom of my mouth hit the floor: she had a toddler on her lap…who was the spitting image of me.

"His name is Michael. He is your son," she said.

"His name is MICHAEL?!?" I was enraged, but held it together in front of the boy.

"Mike came here this morning. I was awakened by the sound of him thrashing your car. He banged on the door, pushing the little one inside, saying, 'Tell Travis he wins again.' Then he began to drag Denise to his car by her hair. I tried to get Michael in the house as fast as I could, so he wouldn't see what was happening."

With tears in my eyes, I picked up my boy. He looked just like me, except he had Denise's nose. I looked at Jasmine and said, "Baby, I didn't know." Crying she embraced us and said, "Travis you don't have to explain, I know you. We are going to be just fine," she said as she kissed Michael's forehead. Looking me in my eyes, she repeated herself, "Just fine."

Even though my world had just turned on its head, I repeated what she said in my spirit; *Just fine indeed.*

GET THE POETRY BOOKS

"A LIGHT SHINES THROUGH DARKNESS"

&

"CRACKS IN MY PALMS"

ON AMAZON.COM NOW!

Made in the USA
Middletown, DE
25 May 2017